From the Files of

Read all the books about Madison Finn!

Coming Soon!

From the Files of

Madison Finn

Give and Take

By Laura Dower

HYPERION
New York

For Nana, the real Gramma Helen

Special thanks to Laura Wilson at the Alzheimer's
Association for her guidance.

Text copyright © 2002 by Laura Dower

From the Files of Madison Finn, Volo, and the Volo colophon are trade-
marks of Disney Enterprises, Inc.

Printed in the United States of America

First Edition
5 7 9 10 8 6 4

The main body of text of this book is set in 13-point Frutiger Roman.

ISBN 0-7868-1684-8

Visit www.madisonfinn.com

Chapter 1

<MadFinn>: r u singing a solo @ the
    Winter concert?

Madison Finn was in a chat room with her two
BFFs, Fiona Waters and Aimee Gillespie. Even though
they had walked home together from school, there
was still lots to discuss.

<Balletgrl>: Fiona, u have an
    excellent voice OF COURSE you'll
    get a solo
<Wetwinz>: so does Poison Ivy
<MadFinn>: maybe you'll both have
    solos
<Balletgrl>: Fiona, I heard Egg is
    singing :-)

<Wetwinz>: so?

<Balletgrl>: singing a love duet with U??? HA HA

<MadFinn>: THAT would be TOOC

<Wetwinz>: im so embarrassed

<MadFinn>: ;-)

<Wetwinz>: let's change the subject pleeeez

<MadFinn>: when's the Nutcracker, Aim?

<Balletgrl>: the day B4 Christmas Eve

<MadFinn>: I wish I could see it but I have 2 go w/my Dad for Christmas and over the vacation week

<Balletgrl>: no biggie I am only playing a snowflake and a candycane, not the lead or n e thing

<Wetwinz>: those are great parts!

<Balletgrl>: maddie when r u leaving?

<MadFinn>: Monday after school gets out I think

<Balletgrl>: we have to hang out a lot ooops G2R

<MadFinn>: huh

<Balletgrl>: Dean needs the computer I have to get off right now sorry bye

```
<Wetwinz>: CUL8R Aim
<Balletgrl>: *poof*
<Wetwinz>: I better go do homework
   too see ya maddie
<MadFinn>: ok C U at school
   tomorrow
```

Madison didn't want to log out of the chat room with her friends, but she signed off after Fiona signed off, hit the STANDBY hot key on her keyboard, and rolled over onto her bed to think.

She had a lot to think about. The Winter Jubilee concert was going to be fun. The holidays were coming. And best of all, Madison was going skiing with Dad.

He'd promised to take her along with him on a real winter vacation to Mount Robinson, a peak in upstate New York. They'd gone once before for a day trip years ago when Mom and Dad were still married. Mom skied the expert trails while Madison and Dad hung out on the bunny slope.

Since the Big D (divorce), Madison had to alternate holidays between her two parents. Madison knew that going away together with Dad would make up for a few of the weekly dinners he had missed lately. Even Mom thought a ski trip was a great idea.

Clicking back onto her laptop, Madison opened her e-mailbox. The only e-mails there were spam—

junk e-mail. Somehow she had been added to a promotional mailing list, receiving e-mail from different girls' catalogs and Web sites. Dad always said that Madison shouldn't open e-mail from strangers because it could download viruses onto her computer. She always followed his advice.

DELETE. DELETE. DELETE.

Madison was sad to see no e-mail from her long-distance keypal Bigwheels. No e-mail from any of her friends. And no e-mail from Dad either, confirming details of the ski trip, like Madison had hoped.

She opened up the special calendar software that helped her to organize her time, after-school meetings, homework, volunteering, and more. As usual, Madison's schedule was jam-packed. December had something to do typed in for almost every day of the month.

```
12/5 Wednesday. Math test. Chorus
   rehearsal.
12/6 Thursday. Science lab w/Ivy.
12/7 Friday. Chorus!!! Work on
   essay. Help Mom decorate.
12/8 Saturday.  Hockey game @
   school.
```

She scrolled down and filled in additional chorus rehearsal dates. Winter Jubilee practices would probably be taking up most of Madison's time over the next few weeks, but she didn't mind. Winter Jubilee was one of the most anticipated weeks of the school year.

"Maddie," Mom said, entering Madison's room without knocking. "I saw you left me this permission slip on the kitchen counter."

Students participating in Winter Jubilee activities needed to have parental approval if they were going to be taken off the school premises. Mom signed on the dotted line and handed it over.

"Thanks, Mom," Madison said, taking the slip.

"By the way," Mom said, sitting down on the edge of Madison's bed, "did you finish that essay you were working on?"

Madison shrugged. "Not really. I'm doing something else right now."

"Fun . . ." Mom asked, eyebrows arched, "or for school?"

Phin, Madison's pug, waddled over to the bed and put his paws up on the edge. Madison reached down to pet his little back.

"Both, Mom," Madison said. "You know I use the laptop for homework and a bunch of other stuff."

"Well, the dog needs to go out," Mom said. "Why don't you take a little break from the 'stuff' and walk him around the block."

As soon as he heard the words *out* and *walk*, Phin jumped off the bed and started to chase his tail. Madison flopped back onto the bed.

"Do I have to?" she groaned.

Mom made a face. "Get up, honey bear. Now. Before he pees on your . . ."

"Okay, okay!" Madison said. "You don't have to be all gross about it."

Mom laughed and handed over the dog leash.

"Rowrooooo!" Phin howled, jumping up into the air on all fours as if he had springs on the bottom of each paw.

Madison laced up her sneakers and grabbed a warmer sweater for herself and for Phin. The pug squirmed as Madison tugged on a green knit cover-up Gramma Helen had knit for him the year before. He looks like a cross between dog and leprechaun, Madison thought as she pushed his paws through.

"Don't stay out too long," Mom cautioned. "It's starting to get even colder outside. And wear that scarf around your head, please."

"Mom, don't be such a worrywart," Madison said.

"I worry. I'm your mom," Mom said, grinning. "Speaking of worrying, did your father call you to confirm the ski plans for the end of December?"

"Plans?" Madison said, thinking fast. "Yes. Well, he e-mailed me actually. Today. He e-mailed me to say the trip was all planned and I shouldn't worry, so neither should you."

Madison gulped. That was a lie. He hadn't e-mailed.

She'd never lied to Mom before.

"So when are you leaving?" Mom asked, leaning back onto Madison's bed.

"L-l-leaving?" Madison stammered. "You mean to take Phinnie out?"

Mom laughed. "No, honey bear. To go *skiing*. When is your Dad taking you away?"

Madison's stomach flip-flopped. She'd lied once. Now she needed to lie twice?

"Gee . . . I don't remember exactly, Mom. Right before Christmas sometime," Madison said. "Like he told us before. You know. What he said."

"Oh," Mom said nonchalantly. "I guess it was unfair of me to assume your Dad would just propose these big plans and . . . well, I won't say it."

"What?" Madison asked. "What were you going to say?"

"No, no. I won't say anything more about your dad."

"Say it," Madison sighed. "I've heard it before."

Mom looked taken aback. "Excuse me?" she said.

"Sorry. I didn't mean to snap like that," Madison said.

"Well, honey bear," Mom said slowly. "I just don't want to see you get your hopes up for some great vacation and then have him change the plans. "

"Oh, Mom," Madison said. "You don't understand. That isn't what's happening this time at all."

"Are you sure? Because sometimes your father—"

"*Please* don't worry," Madison said, cutting off her mother midthought. "Everything will be fine. Dad and I will have an awesome winter vacation and everything will be perfect . . . except that you won't be there."

Mom smiled. "Thanks, sweetheart. I'll miss you too."

"Rowrrooooooo!" Phinnie wailed. He scratched at his ears and belly. The green sweater itched and he wanted O-U-T. Madison was happier than happy that the dog was acting up. It provided the best distraction.

She clipped on Phin's leash and walked down the stairs, out the front door, and into the cold.

The pair wandered down the block at a slow pace. The air was so cold that Madison could feel her toes through her shoes and socks. Phin could see his doggy breath. Madison's wool scarf helped keep out the chilly wind.

After a few moments, Madison found herself walking past Aimee's house. Her BFF lived only a few houses down from Madison on Blueberry Road. Sometimes Madison would stop by on her walks around the neighborhood.

She climbed up the doorstep and rang the doorbell. It played a few bars of Beethoven. Mr. Gillespie loved classical music, even on his doorbell.

"Maddie! What are you doing here?" Aimee said when she opened the door. She bent down to scratch behind Phin's ears.

"Do you want to go for a walk with me and Phin?" she asked. "And Blossom, of course." Blossom was Aimee's basset hound who hated the cold weather but loved Phinnie.

Aimee slipped on her parka. "Let's go!" she said.

Phin and Blossom sniffed each other hello while their walkers walked, talking some more about the school concert, Ivy, and homework. Aimee had been in the middle of finishing her science homework when Madison arrived.

"I have too much to do," Aimee complained.

Madison nodded in agreement. "Me, too."

"And I think science class is such a drag," Aimee said.

Madison agreed. "Me, too."

"And I wish it would snow," Aimee said with a sigh. "Winter isn't winter without snow and ice. The cold isn't the same. Know what I mean?"

"It sort of smells like snow," Madison said.

"I'd give anything to go skiing over vacation like you," Aimee said. "Instead, I'm stuck at home hanging out with my dumb brothers."

Madison shrugged. "Yeah, I'm psyched. I haven't been to Mount Robinson for a long time."

"And it's in Longmont, which is such a cool town," Aimee said. "They have this store with hand-made ballet shoes. I remember because my mom took me there for my birthday one year. Remember? I'd give anything to go back there again."

"I'd give anything to—" Madison started to say, but she cut herself off. She sniffed the cold air and walked a few paces ahead with Phin.

"Hey, Maddie, wait up!" Aimee yelled. She and Blossom ran to catch up. "You didn't tell me. What are you wishing for this holiday?"

Madison considered sharing her *real* wish, a secret one about Mom and Dad getting back together. But she didn't. Instead she yelled up to the sky.

"SNOW!" Madison bellowed. "SNOOOOOOOOW!"

"You're the best," Aimee said, laughing.

The two friends locked arms and continued their walk around the block.

Chapter 2

"Sit over here!" Fiona yelled, waving to Madison and Aimee as they entered the chorus rehearsal room.

Madison glanced around. Most of the seventh grade had shown up for the first official Winter Jubilee singing practice. The entire class would sing at the final events; but kids were only required to attend a few rehearsals before then. Many students had afternoon conflicts with other clubs and teams.

Aimee nudged Madison. "Don't look now, but—" Aimee groaned.

"Hello, Madison," Ivy Daly said. She edged past and sat in the row directly behind Madison and her friends. The drones followed. Madison could feel the enemy breathing behind her.

The feud between Madison and her friends and Ivy and her drones had lasted for more than three years and showed no signs of slowing. It didn't take much to fuel bad feelings among the girls: a funny look, a long stare, or even a Winter Jubilee choral rehearsal.

"Don't say hello, why don't you?" Rose Thorn snickered.

Madison ignored her.

Mrs. Montefiore clapped her hands and tapped her music stand. As several students helped pass around copies of sheet music, Mrs. Montefiore read through the list of songs they'd be singing.

"Silver Bells"
"You're a Mean One, Mr. Grinch"
"Winter Wonderland"
"Dreidel, Dreidel, Dreidel"
"Stopping by Woods on a Snowy Evening"

"The Grinch song should be for *them*," Fiona whispered, indicating the row where Ivy and the drones were sitting.

Madison stifled a giggle. "Just ignore them," she said.

"Hey! Where's Adam Sandler's Hanukkah song?" Aimee said, cracking herself up.

"ATTENTION!" Mrs. Montefiore yelled.

Tap, tap, tap, tap, tap.

The music teacher steadied her conductor's baton and shot a glare over in the girls's direction. She explained the week's schedule of events for Winter Jubilee; asked the kids to sing a few scales; and led the entire room in a quick review of each song's first verse. Madison faked it, mouthing the words. She wanted to be a part of everything but she wasn't a great singer. So she decided she'd be a part of everything silently.

Fiona, on the other hand, sang like a pop star. Madison knew that the drones had to be jealous of Fiona's voice. During the first part of "Winter Wonderland," when Fiona hit all the high notes perfectly, Madison swore she heard Rose and Joanie cough. Sabotage! Sometimes the drones were even more obnoxious than their leader.

Their leader, Poison Ivy, didn't say much. But Madison guessed Ivy was too busy singing herself to make fun of anyone else. Not only was Ivy the seventh-grade class president, top student, and all-around popular girl, but she could sing like a pop star, too.

After running through the song list once, and watching the clock for an hour, the seventh graders gave themselves a roaring round of applause. As everyone gathered their book bags to leave, Mrs. Montefiore invited Señora Diaz up to the front of the rehearsal room.

"You are not dismissed!" Mrs. Montefiore commanded the students. Everyone sank back down into their chairs.

13

Señora Diaz was Madison's friend Egg's mother. Ever since she was little Madison had known Señora Diaz. Now Madison was even in Señora Diaz's Spanish class at Far Hills Junior High. Madison wasn't an A+ Spanish student, but she wasn't failing either. As usual, she was somewhere in the middle.

"Hola!" Señora Diaz greeted everyone with a grin. "I have an exciting volunteer project to tell you about, over at The Estates, a nursing home in town. I spoke to my sister who is a nurse at the home and she suggested that some members of our chorus might be interested in doing volunteer work there."

A girl in the front row raised her hand. "Do you mean more singing?"

"No, Señorita," Señora Diaz continued. "We are looking for a small group of students willing to give up a few afternoons from now until the holidays in an Adopt-a-Grandparent program. Students will keep company with senior citizens whose families live far away."

"Are these people *sick*?" some boy yelled from the back row.

"Not like YOU!" Chet said, louder than he meant to. He covered his mouth and apologized.

"To answer your question," Señora Diaz said, "some people are sick with diseases, while others are just lonely."

Everyone started whispering again. The room got noisy in seconds.

"STUDENTS, PLEASE!" Mrs. Montefiore yelled, tapping her baton, her voice booming through the din. All at once, the room hushed.

"I'm going to put a sign-up sheet right here on the desk," Señora Diaz continued. "And I'd like both boys and girls to sign up. Remember that you need to have some solid free time to do this. After-school activities will be a conflict for some of you, but I do hope the rest will consider helping out."

Madison's brain was already buzzing. She could sign up to volunteer! She loved to volunteer! She could make time to adopt a grandparent! It would be fun to spread a little holiday cheer.

Plus, Madison thought, it would be great to volunteer with Fiona and Aimee.

Before she could maneuver her way out of the row of seats, however, Madison watched Ivy and her drones rush the front desk and the sign-up sheet. Ivy stopped to say something to Señora Diaz.

"Hurry," Madison said. "Move, Aimee."

"What is your rush?" Aimee asked. "I'm getting my stuff."

"I want us to get to the sign-up sheet. I don't think anyone has signed up yet and the three of us have to do it together—" Madison said, climbing over her friend.

"The three of us?" Fiona said. "Wait. Maddie, I can't volunteer."

Madison stopped short. "You can't?"

"Neither can I," said Aimee.

"I have soccer," Fiona said.

"And I have ballet," Aimee said.

"Oh, yeah," Madison sighed. "Of course. I forgot."

"Why don't you go sign up by yourself?" Aimee asked. "You like doing that kind of stuff. That would be cool if you volunteered at The Estates."

Madison shrugged. "Yeah, I guess. But by myself?"

Aimee and Fiona lingered by while Madison approached the sign-up sheet. Egg and Hart were standing nearby.

"Hey, Finnster," Hart said, calling Madison by a name he'd made up years earlier. "You signing up?"

Hart was Madison's junior-high crush: cute, smart, and silly. Madison couldn't take her eyes off him.

"I think so," Madison said, looking for a pencil in her orange bag. "Are you guys signing up?"

"Well, my *tía* Ana, the one who's a nurse, is super cool," Egg explained. "So I figured it would be a good thing to help her out. I mean, I've got hockey practice, but my mom is bugging me to do it, so . . ."

"What about you, Hart?" Madison asked.

"Yeah, I'm doing it with Egg," he said, smiling. "Our hockey coach said that we can miss one or two practices and still play in the game next Saturday."

That was all Madison needed to hear. She smiled back and leaned forward to add her name to the list. Even though Fiona and Aimee had been Madison's first hope to join her at The Estates, Egg and Hart would be just as entertaining company.

The list was almost filled. The name at the very top was "Hilary Klein," a girl in Madison's English class who always dressed up in matched sweater sets and frilly socks; carried a purse in addition to her book bag; and applied eyeliner in the girls' room between classes. She wasn't very friendly, so Madison wasn't quite sure why *she* would volunteer to be some stranger's friend. But there she was.

Underneath Hilary's name were those of Hart, Egg, Davy Miller, and Joey O'Neill, nose-picker extraordinaire.

Then, in giant letters, was the name Ivy Daly, with a curlicue on the *y*. Madison groaned. Although she didn't want to spend free afternoons with the enemy, she added her own name under Ivy's.

After leaving the chorus room, Madison headed to the lockers to retrieve her social studies textbook and some other papers. Fiona and Aimee were waiting there.

"Now the three of us can walk home together," Aimee said. She had on her lemon-colored parka with a furry white crocheted hat and gloves.

"I think it's cool that you volunteered," Fiona said. She wore a baseball cap that read ANGELS, and a jean jacket with a sheepskin lining. She'd wrapped her scarf all around her braids and neck.

"Yeah, it's cool. Except for Ivy," Madison said. She pulled her quilted winter jacket out of her locker and zipped up the front. "Let's go," she told her BFFs.

They headed out the school doors toward home.

As Madison approached her house, Phin saw her and made a dash for the sidewalk. But the pug couldn't reach. He was tethered to a post in the front yard, wearing his green sweater, of course.

"Hey, Mom!" Madison called out. Mom was bent over a hedge by the porch, wrapping it in preparation for snow.

"Hey, honey bear!" Mom said, tying knotted rope around a wide piece of burlap. "Come and help me, would you?"

Madison skipped over to the porch and dropped her bag. She couldn't wait to tell Mom about her new volunteering gig at The Estates.

Mom had other questions on her mind.

"Did you check your e-mail today?" Mom asked.

Madison nodded. "Yeah. Why?"

"I was just wondering when your father is going to firm up those Christmas plans. He said he would e-mail you right away, didn't he? I need to make reservations for myself and I can't do it unless I know you're going to be safe and sound somewhere with Dad. Did he e-mail?"

Madison squirmed. "Well, I don't know what's happening."

"What?" Mom said. "You told me yesterday that he confirmed all the plans and dates. Now we were waiting for him to—"

"Waiting!" Madison said. "Oh yeah. Well that's true. I am waiting for . . . for . . ."

"ROWROOOOOO!" Phin let out a howl. His leash was wound all around the post in the yard. Mom ran over to unwind him. Madison took advantage of the break in the interrogation.

"I'm going inside, Mom, okay?"

"Okay," Mom said. "We'll talk about this later."

Madison hurried into the front hallway. She checked the message machine first, hoping that she'd find a recorded greeting from Dad. But the only message was a garbled one from Gramma Helen. That happened sometimes when Gramma called from her cell phone out near Lake Michigan.

Fzzzzzzzzzt. Love you. Szzzzzzbpp. Bye-bye. Kkkkkchk.

With no greeting from Dad on the machine, Madison started to worry. She plugged in her laptop and modem, looking for a message from Dad, entering bigfishbowl.com with fingers and toes crossed.

NEW MAIL.

Madison gasped when she saw three new messages blinking inside her e-mailbox. There were notes from Gramma, Fiona, and DAD!

FROM	SUBJECT
✉ GoGramma	Missing You
✉ Wetwinz	Fw: Re: Chorus
✉ JeffFinn	Vacation

Madison opened Dad's mail first.

```
From: JeffFinn
To: MadFinn
Subject: Vacation
Date: Wed 5 Dec 1:24 PM
```
I'm off to a big meeting, but I
just wanted to check in with my
one and only. How is school? You
must be excited about the upcoming
vacation. Can't wait to see you.

Here's a joke for you.

What happened when the ice monster
had a fight with the zombie? He
gave him the cold shoulder! LOL.

Thinking of you all the time. I
love you.

Dad

Madison reread Dad's e-mail twice more just to make sure she hadn't missed anything. This was the vacation confirmation Madison had been waiting for

. . . wasn't it? She wasn't sure. The only thing certain in this e-mail was the standard bad Dad joke.

What was Madison supposed to tell Mom now?

She hit SAVE and moved along to the other messages.

Fiona's note was simple. She had a few boring questions about the chorus schedule.

Gramma Helen's message was a little longer. She was "checking in on her family." Madison read the e-mail and hit REPLY.

From: MadFinn
To: GoGramma
Subject: I Have Super Big NEWS
Date: Wed 5 Dec 5:01 PM

Thanks for your nice note, Gramma. Mom and I are fine. We got your voice message too but it was all static. You have to get a new phone, I think.

I have the coolest news about school. Remember I told you about the chorus and Winter Jubilee at FHJH? Well, I'm also going to be a volunteer at this place in Far Hills called The Estates. It's for older people (older than you, though, because I don't really think you're old!). But the funny part is

21

that the program is called Adopt-a-Grandparent, so how could I not remember you! I hope you don't mind if I'm standing in as an adopted granddaughter for someone else. I wonder what everyone there will want to talk about? I may be calling or e-mailing you for ideas, Gramma. I love you so much. How is life by the lake? I hope I can come visit you sometime soon. Are you excited about Christmas?

Love you lots,

Maddie

As Madison hit SEND, she felt teeny butterflies inside her belly. Although vacation was still a little undecided, she sensed that this Christmas season just might turn out special in some way.

She just wasn't sure *how*.

There was a long—and hopefully snowy—road ahead.

Chapter 3

 Winter Break

Please let there be SNOW. Lots of it. I went through my entire closet last night after dinner and pulled out all the clothes I could find for skiing. I wish I could go shopping for more, but I can't. My sweaters are getting soooo stretched out. Maybe Dad will take me to the mall once he makes the final plans for our trip? I hope that's sooner than soon.

Mom woke up this morning and asked me about the vacation again at breakfast. Arrgh! I pretended I didn't hear. I know that Dad might change the vacation plans because he does that sometimes. But the thing is, I can deal with it. What I CAN'T

deal with is the way Mom feels about Dad
when he does that.

Mom and Dad are so nice to each other
all year long and then at Christmas, why
does it get awkward and angry and YUCK?
It's just one of those things that bugs me
since they got divorced.

The weather forecast says we might
get up to twenty inches of snow on the
mountains outside Far Hills. Isn't that
wild? And even if I won't be enjoying the
ski slopes with Dad, I won't get bummed
out like Mom thinks.

Rude Awakening: Snow news isn't always
good news. But I'm *still* looking forward
to my winter break.

Madison saved her file onto a disk, leaned back in
her chair, and glanced around the room. She and
Fiona came up to the library media center during
their last free period to do homework. Madison was
falling behind in social studies class and owed her
teacher a few chapter reviews. At least, that was
what she was trying to work on. In reality, she
wasn't writing about the American Revolution. She was
writing in her files.

"Maddie," Fiona said, distracted from her homework, too. "Do you . . . do you think Egg likes me?"

Madison looked over from her computer terminal. "Yes, Fiona. How many times are you going to
ask me that? And Aimee thinks so too."

Fiona giggled. "Sorry."

"Are you blushing?" Madison asked. She giggled too.

The bell rang indicating that the free period had ended. Fiona shoved her papers into her bag.

"Should I ask him out?" Fiona asked.

Madison shook her head. "Absolutely not. Wait for him to ask you."

"But that's *so* twentieth-century," Fiona said, grinning.

"Yeah, I know. We're supposed to be in charge of our destinies and all that. At least that's what my Mom says all the time. But Egg will get all weird if you ask him first. Not because he's a boy. Just because he gets weird about everything. Trust me," Madison said. She'd known Egg since they were little kids.

"Okay," Fiona said with a shrug and hurried toward the door. "I have to go to soccer now. E-mail me later, okay?"

Madison nodded and pulled her own books together. She had to dash, too. She was meeting Señora Diaz and the rest of the Adopt-a-Grandparent volunteers in room 306, the Spanish classroom.

She raced down to the room, almost slamming right into Egg and Hart on the way inside.

"Where's the fire?" Egg cracked.

Madison frowned. "Whatever, Egg. Can I please get by?"

Egg smiled back. "Sure, if you can fit." He and Hart blocked the doorway.

Madison stood back with her hands on her hips. "What is up with you?" Madison asked. She couldn't believe that Fiona liked one of these guys. Then again, Madison couldn't believe that *she* liked one of these guys, too.

"Excuse me," Ivy Daly said as she came up from behind Madison. "Is there a reason why you guys are holding up everything?"

Madison turned to Ivy. "I'm with you," she said, not believing the words as they came out of her mouth. "Move it, Egg."

Unbelieveably, Ivy *smiled*. "Yeah."

Egg and Hart rushed in and sat down.

Madison scanned the colorful ceiling and walls of the small room. They were covered in posters of Spain and Puerto Rico. Señora Diaz had also hung red, yellow, and blue streamers everywhere.

Chairs were arranged in a semicircle, and everyone had their book bags lying around on chairs and on the floor, so it was hard to find the right empty seat to sit in. For a split second Madison stood there, frozen, not knowing what to do.

But a lot can happen in a split second.

"Let's just sit there," Ivy suggested, pointing to the chair nearest to Hart.

Madison's eyes got very wide. "There?"

"Duh," Ivy said. "Where else?"

Duh was right. Ivy had never in the history of junior high asked Madison to sit with her; and Madison was dumbstruck. Should she sit with Ivy or not?

Madison quickly weighed her options. She could sit near Davy Miller, who smelled, or Joey O'Neill, who picked his nose.

One of the other Adopt-a-Grandparent volunteers, Hilary Klein, was seated across the room. Madison briefly considered sitting with her . . . but decided against that, too. Everyone in the seventh grade knew Hilary was the class brainiac—but she wasn't very friendly. She and her clique kept to themselves, usually in the library. Plus, she was staring.

"Can we please make a sitting decision," Ivy said, pushing in front of Madison.

"Okay, over here is great," Madison said to Ivy, dragging herself over to the empty seats Ivy had indicated before. Ivy plopped down into the chair nearest to Hart—of course. Madison squeezed in on the other side.

"I can't believe you're volunteering for this," Egg said to Madison.

"Yeah, well, so are you," she replied.

"Only because I HAVE to do it, I told you that," Egg said.

"I don't believe you, Egg. You like doing this stuff. Admit it," Madison said.

"It'll be cool," Hart said.

27

Madison smiled at him. "Yeah, cool."

"Totally cool," Ivy blurted.

"Yeah, well then you guys can be cool. I'm telling you that if it wasn't for my *tía* Ana and my mother—"

Egg stopped speaking because Señora Diaz had just walked into her room, carrying a pile of purple folders. She handed a folder to each student in the room.

"*Hola, estudiantes!*" Señora Diaz said cheerfully.

"*Hola*," everyone replied, including Egg.

Señora Diaz explained that each member of the small group of Adopt-a-Grandparent volunteers would be assigned to a specific resident of The Estates. Names of boys and girls had been matched randomly to men and women living in the home. Since each resident had requested a holiday "friend," the student's job was to keep that person company, chat, get snacks, and do whatever else they wanted to do together. The only catch was that some of the older people were dealing with certain illnesses. Señora Diaz wanted to make sure this would not be problematic for any of the kids.

"How sick is sick?" Ivy asked aloud.

"That's a very good question, señorita. The truth is, sickness depends on the person. I know one gentleman on our list is in a wheelchair. Another woman can barely see because she has cataracts in her eyes. And a couple of the residents have been diagnosed with Alzheimer's disease—in its early stages."

"Oh, man, what's *that*?" Davy Miller said.

Egg and Hart laughed, but shut up quickly. Señora Diaz was shaking her head.

"Is something funny, Walter? Boys, this is no laughing matter. Alzheimer's starts out as minor memory loss, forgetfulness, and other symptoms. As the disease progresses, the symptoms get worse and worse. Sometimes the man or woman forgets more serious things."

"Like what?" Hilary asked.

"Like what they were doing yesterday. Or who they are. Or who *you* are," Señora Diaz explained. "But don't worry. We will have a meeting after every afternoon at The Estates to discuss what happened that day. That gives everyone a chance to talk about your experience. If you feel in any way uncomfortable, you can switch your visits or stop altogether."

"You mean I could be hanging with some old dude one minute and then the next time I show up he won't even remember me?" Davy asked.

Señora Diaz sighed. "Yes, David. That is what I mean. Thank you for explaining that so eloquently."

Davy shrunk down into his seat.

The group reviewed a bunch of other procedures and rules about visiting The Estates and discussed the schedule for departure from school the very next day. They would meet downstairs in the school lobby, board the school minivan, and arrive at The Estates at three o'clock. Madison counted eight volunteers altogether, including herself and Hart. She was determined to get a seat near her crush for that ride. Hopefully Ivy wouldn't get there first.

Mom wasn't home when Madison arrived on the porch. She'd left a note.

Went for supper. Back by 5. Phin already went out.
How was your day? Luv, Mom
P.S. Call your Dad

Without Mom to pester her about staying on the computer too long, Madison hurried upstairs to log onto the laptop from behind her bedroom door with its DO NOT DISTURB sign. She had just enough time before Mom got back home to swim around online at big-fishbowl.com. Madison needed to check her e-mailbox and see if anyone from her buddy list was there, too.

Her keypal Bigwheels wasn't online. Neither was Fiona nor Aimee.

Egg was online, but Madison didn't feel like talking to him.

In the middle of reading her list, Madison got an Insta-Message.

From Dad.

```
<JeffFinn>: Maddie online? Hip hip
<MadFinn>: Hooray!
```

After waiting to hear from him for so long,

Madison was relieved to know he was finally calling about the ski trip. She had so many questions to ask.

What should she pack? How much snow had fallen on Mount Robinson? When were they leaving?

```
<JeffFinn>: I want to know if you
    still want to spend Christmastime
    together
<MadFinn>: OF COURSE!!! What do you
    think Dad? I've been waiting to
    hear
<JeffFinn>: Good. I want to spend
    it with you too. There's been a
    little change in our plan, just a
    little
<MadFinn>: change
<JeffFinn>: we can't go ski that's
    all
<MadFinn>: oh
<JeffFinn>: are you disappointed? I
    know u must be
<MadFinn>: not really
```

Madison lied to Dad, too. She didn't know what else to say.

```
<JeffFinn>: I just can't get away
    for a whole week and Stephanie
    will be around
<MadFinn>: Stephanie?
```

31

Madison's heart sank a little more. Stephanie was Dad's girlfriend, and ever since they'd been dating, Madison had always felt a little bit jealous. Stephanie rode in the front seat all the time—where Madison used to sit. Stephanie sat near Dad when they ate at restaurants or went to the movies. Stephanie was the last person Dad thought of every night. At least Madison guessed all that was true.

```
<JeffFinn>: IMS are you there?
<MadFinn>: yes
<JeffFinn>: I know you were looking
   forward to this trip
<MadFinn>: a little
<JeffFinn>: m(_)m
<MadFinn>: whatever Dad NP
```

Madison couldn't share her true feelings—especially not in a chat room or on an Insta-Message board.

She'd considered the idea that Dad might cancel the trip, but hearing him actually *do it* didn't help the sadness Madison felt inside. Had Mom been right about Dad? Why did Madison expect the best when everyone else thought the worst? What was Dad's problem?

```
<JeffFinn>: Maddie, we can go skiing
   another time
```

```
<MadFinn>: ok fine
<JeffFinn>: can we talk about this
   more later on in person?
<MadFinn>: ok fine
<JeffFinn>: are you okay?
<MadFinn>: ok
<JeffFinn>: fine. Can I call later?
<MadFinn>: yeah BNN
```

Madison signed off and scanned the buddy list again. She searched for Bigwheels in all the chat rooms, but Bigwheels was *still* nowhere to be found.

Why wasn't her keypal online? Madison sent e-mail right away.

```
From: MadFinn
To: Bigwheels
Subject: Ski Trip
Date: Thurs 6 Dec 4:08 PM
I wrote a day or so ago asking if
you knew how to ski. Well, ignore
that one. I'm not going on a ski
trip of any kind. My dad bailed!!!
Mom will probably freak out on him.
That is no fun to watch.

Do you have any advice 4 me? Ur
parents argue a lot too--right?
What r they like when they fight?
Do they scream and put you in the
middle of the whole mess or do they
```

leave you out of everything? My parents do all those things but mostly they pretend to be nice when I know they really don't mean it. It's so confusing. And it's the holidays. Which means more fights to come. HELP.

I am sad about missing the skiing trip but how do I get my mom to be nice to my dad? How would you deal?

Yours till the ski lifts,

Maddie

P.S. All is NOT lost for Christmas b/c I'm volunteering at this nursing home and singing in chorus. So I am keeping busier than busy. U know me. WBS.

Somewhere downstairs, the front door slammed. Madison jumped so suddenly that Phin started to howl.

"Maddie?" Mom called out. "Are you home yet?"

Madison gulped. "Mom?" she said weakly. "I'm up here."

Madison prepped herself for speaking to Mom.

She would dump the bad news and accept the consequences. Simple. Mom could handle it calmly.

"I've had the worst day," Mom groaned as she climbed the stairs to Madison's bedroom. "The worst day in a long, long time. How about you? Could it get any worse?"

Madison gulped.

She was NOT telling Mom about the canceled ski trip.

At least not tonight.

Chapter 4

By the time Friday afternoon rolled around, Madison had nearly forgotten about Dad's bad news. She still hadn't mentioned the canceled trip to Mom.

All she could think about now was The Estates. The very first visit to the nursing home was this afternoon. Señora Diaz's volunteers were excused early from their other classes to go meet the minivan.

Madison and Ivy left science class early together along with Hart. Walking down the silent corridor, Madison felt like she was in an episode of the *Twilight Zone*. Not because it was dark and creepy, but because it was so strange.

Ivy was talking to Madison instead of Hart?

"What do you think your person at The Estates will be like?" Ivy asked Madison, flipping her red hair as she spoke.

"Nice, I hope," Madison said.

"I hope I don't get someone who's sick," Ivy said, talking fast. "I mean, I guess I'll deal with it if I do, but I'd rather have someone who wants to walk around and talk a lot and not just sit there."

"I'm sure you'll like whoever you get," Madison said.

Ivy smiled again. "Yeah, I guess you're right."

Madison wanted to grab Ivy by the shoulders and ask her what was going on. Why was the enemy being so friendly?

Hart just walked along in a daze. "I am so tired," he said. "Hockey practice is killing me. And I have a game tomorrow."

"I'm going to the game with Aimee and Fiona," Madison said, smiling.

"I'm going, too," Ivy said.

Madison shrugged as if she didn't know what Ivy was saying. Luckily, Hart kept changing the subject.

"The coach had me doing skating drills yesterday after school," Hart said. "My left knee hurts."

"Why did you sign up to do volunteer work if you're so busy with hockey?" Madison asked him.

"Because," Hart answered, "it's Christmas and my Ya Ya, my grandmother, said I should. It's the right thing to do. And because Egg begged me to do it with him."

"Oh," Madison said, a little disappointed by Hart's answer. She'd been hoping he would say something about wanting to save the world.

37

"I'm doing it because I'm class president and I'm supposed to do these kinds of things," Ivy said in a loud voice, strutting along. She flipped her hair again.

"Why are you doing it, Maddie?" Hart asked.

"Because she's little Miss Do Everything," Ivy said.

"No," Madison corrected her. "I want to do it."

"Whatever you say, Maddie," Ivy said.

"I like to volunteer. Sometimes I volunteer at the animal clinic. I helped my mom once serve at a soup kitchen. And it's Christmas now. We're supposed to do stuff like this. Señora Diaz said some of these people at The Estates have no families of their own."

"I know," Ivy said, sounding a little more sympathetic.

Madison was sure she hadn't heard Ivy agree with her in a long time. She'd add that tidbit of information to her "Ivy" file when she got home.

"Over here!" Señora Diaz called out as the trio reached the school lobby. The other kids from their volunteer group were gathered together in a huddle except for Egg, who was missing.

Señora Diaz tapped her foot impatiently. "Does anyone know where Walter is?" she asked.

As if on cue, Egg jumped out from behind a bank of lockers. He leaped in front of the group with a bold "Ta-da!"

A few kids laughed, but Señora Diaz frowned

and pushed him toward the school exit. "Follow us," she told the rest of the group. The corners of her mouth got all scrunched up as if she was about to spit. "Next time, we have to get to the lobby on time, don't we, Walter?"

Egg just sighed. "Yes, Señora Diaz." He often called his mother that when they were at school. As silly or as angry as Egg got, and as much as Señora Diaz could push his buttons, Egg tried not to disrespect his mother in the school building.

Everyone rushed the van and took their seats.

Hart and Egg sat in the middle with Joey O'Neill, who didn't seem to care much where he sat or who he sat with. Davy sat in the back row behind Hilary Klein. She wasn't too happy about that one. She had to plug her nose during most of the ride. A fourth girl named Monica Rizzo sat across the aisle from Hilary.

Once again, Madison and Ivy faced a seating dilemma, just like at the meeting. They sat a row apart this time, far enough to have their own "space," but close enough to talk—if they wanted to. Ivy sat closer to Señora Diaz. They would spend the entire ride chatting, Madison guessed. Ivy pretended to be soooo interested in everything their teacher had to say.

Señora Diaz explained how The Estates mansion and guest homes had been built by a rich landowner searching for a sanctuary away from New

York City. Here, it was private and peaceful. Madison looked around as they approached the property. She could understand why people would want to live there. Owners over the years had planted beautiful gardens where visitors and residents could walk around. As the seventh-grade minibus pulled into The Estates cul-de-sac, Madison could see the shallow dirt where rows of flowers would grow in springtime.

Egg's aunt Ana greeted the van with a grin.

"*Hola!*" Ana cried, sounding an awful lot—and looking an awful lot—like her sister, Señora Diaz.

Ana threw her arms around Egg to say hello. His family had always been affectionate like that. Madison knew it embarrassed him.

"*Hola*, Tía Ana," he said softly.

Ana grinned. "I'm glad to see you here."

Davy Miller snickered and Hart elbowed him to shut up.

The group was led through the front doors of The Estates, past two huge potted plants, a pile of suitcases, and a cluster of older people seated in a lounge area. One woman was knitting, a few men were playing cards, and the rest were just staring off into space.

"Look at them," Ivy whispered to Madison. "It's like they're not really there."

"I wonder what they do all day?" Madison wondered aloud. "I would get so bored, I think."

Ana showed the group into a small office with a conference table and sodas. Egg grabbed a Sprite as soon as he sat down. Davy Miller grabbed two.

"First of all," Nurse Ana said, "I want to thank all of you for coming to see us today. I know the group of seniors you will meet is very thrilled to meet you, too. Our activity director, Mr. Lynch, will take you inside and pair you off. Then you and your partner can spend the afternoon together. Sound good? We'll all come back in an hour or so for a little refreshment."

Mr. Lynch came into the room next, followed by a cluster of older men and women. Madison felt her heart beat inside her chest. It was exciting to make a new friend, she thought, no matter what age she was. She stared at every new face.

Everyone waited patiently as Mr. Lynch handed a piece of paper to Señora Diaz. She read the list of pairs slowly.

Hilary Klein was first on the list, which wasn't in any particular order. They placed Hilary with a woman in a wheelchair named Miss Peggy. It appeared that Peggy was shy, so the two of them seemed like a perfect match.

Davy Miller was assigned to a short, round, and very fat man named Mickey, whose last name just also happened to be Miller. Davy seemed to like that coincidence. Madison wondered if maybe Mickey had B.O. like Davy did. That would have been a better coincidence. He gave Mickey the extra Sprite and they walked out into the hall together.

Hart was assigned to a bearded man dressed in a brown suit and tie even though it was by no means a formal occasion. The man said his name was Mr. Leo Koppel. That was all he said. Hart looked nervous, but the man put his hand on Hart's shoulder and they walked out together.

Egg was paired with a man wearing a brown T-shirt who called himself Smokey. He acted very serious because it was the anniversary date of the Pearl Harbor bombing. Madison could hear Smokey mumbling. "December seventh," he said to Egg. "Day of infamy. My cousin Skeeter was there. Never forget him."

"This guy seems pretty cool," Egg said to Madison as he walked out with Smokey. Madison laughed.

Soon, the room was paired off except for Ivy, Madison, and two other women. One older woman had on a bright orange straw hat and a flowered dress even though it was wintertime. The other woman had on a blue-and-white-checked dress, buttoned all the way up to the top, and a fuzzy cardigan sweater. She wasn't smiling at all.

Madison knew immediately who she'd get. The woman with the hat was wearing her favorite color. It was meant to be.

But then Señora Diaz read off Ivy's name. And Ivy

was paired with orange-hat lady, whose real name was Holly. Mrs. Holly Wood. Not only was she cool-looking, but she had the cool name to go with the looks.

Madison got Eleanor Romano and her fuzzy sweater dress instead.

"Hi," Madison said as they walked out into the hall. "I'm Maddie. How are you, Mrs. Romano?"

Mrs. Romano sighed. "My back aches today," she said. "Ana told me I should take on one of you young volunteers to cheer me up, but I don't know that I need any cheering up. I really don't like the holidays much."

Madison froze up. "Oh," she said.

"You have to excuse me. I'm always like this," Mrs. Romano said. "Like I said, my back aches and I just . . . well, I'll try to enjoy myself with you, young lady. What did you say your name was?"

"Madison," she said. "Madison Finn."

"That's a nice name," Mrs. Romano said. "My name is Eleanor Romano."

"I know," Madison said. "That's a nice name, too."

"Oh no, it's a horrid name. I'm named after my crazy Aunt Ellie," she said. "But the truth is, she wasn't really crazy, she was just spirited. I used to be like that. A long, long time ago."

"Oh," Madison said.

"Do you want to go see my room?" Mrs. Romano

asked. "I have flowered walls. It cheers me up in the wintertime especially."

Madison shrugged. "Okay," she said. "Let's go."

"You know," Mrs. Romano said as they walked down the hall toward her room. "You are a very pretty young girl."

Madison beamed. "Thank you," she said. "Mom says I look a lot like my gramma Helen, actually."

"Are you and your grandmother close?" Mrs. Romano asked.

Madison nodded. "Totally. We talk on the phone and e-mail each other a lot."

"You know how to do all those electronic mail gadgets? I could never figure out something like that. I just don't understand how it all works. Computers baffle me."

"It's easy," Madison said. "Maybe I can show you sometime."

"So why are you adopting a grandparent when you already are close to one of your own?" Mrs. Romano asked.

Madison didn't know what to say. She shrugged. "I don't know. I just wanted to volunteer, that's all."

They arrived at Mrs. Romano's room a few moments later. The walls were covered with winding ivy wallpaper and framed pictures of different flowers. In one corner, there were some smaller framed photos of birds lined up in three rows of four across.

"Who are *they*?" Madison asked.

"My children," Mrs. Romano replied. "I've had twelve different birds in my life. Each one has his or her picture up on this wall."

"Wow," Madison said, taking a closer look. "That's nice."

Mrs. Romano smiled. "You're just saying that to be nice yourself. You think I'm a little weird, don't you? There was another kid who volunteered here. He thought I was weird. Called me the bird lady. I got a kick out of that."

"No," Madison said nervously. "I don't think you're weird. I don't think that at all."

In this case, Madison figured it was okay to lie— a little. She didn't want Mrs. Romano to feel bad after they'd just met.

For the next hour, Mrs. Romano showed Madison ten different kinds of birds that lived just outside her big bay window. The room overlooked the rolling lawn outside The Estates. Mrs. Romano said she would sit there all morning and watch the birds eating, flying, and playing.

"I always wished I could fly," Mrs. Romano said. "Wouldn't that be great?"

Madison nodded. "It's almost time to go," she said. "I guess we have to say good-bye."

"I'll walk you back to the lobby," Mrs. Romano said. "I had a good afternoon. Didn't expect to. But you're sweet."

"I had a good time, too," Madison said. "And I'm not just saying that to make you feel better. I really did."

"Well, as a matter of fact, I do feel better. Next time you come, I want you to tell me all about yourself, okay?"

Madison nodded. "Okay."

When she arrived back in the main lobby of The Estates, Mr. Lynch gathered all the volunteers into the room for a meeting. He wanted a report from all the kids about their visits. Madison was surprised to find that everyone had had a positive experience. Even Egg, who said Smokey yelled at him for no reason a few times, enjoyed himself. It was better than anyone had expected. Nurse Ana was pleased, too.

"Mrs. Wood was so funny," Ivy said. "She and I tried on costume jewelry and other stuff all afternoon. She has like forty pairs of shoes in her closet!"

Madison smiled. "Wow, that's really interesting. I wonder if she wears them all."

"So what did you do?" Ivy asked Madison. "Was your lady stuck-up? She looked kind of boring."

"We looked at birds," Madison said. "I mean, it sounds boring, but Mrs. Romano made it fun. Even though she was complaining a little. She was nice. She reminded me of my own grandmother."

"I wish my Grams was half as nice as Mrs. Wood," Ivy said. "Can you believe her name? MY lady was the coolest."

"Yeah, and Holly is a good name for Christmas, too," Madison joked.

Ivy rolled her eyes. "Yeah, yeah. So, when are you coming back here?"

"I guess next week," Madison replied.

"Yeah, me too," Ivy said.

Señora Diaz called everyone together for the minibus, and Ivy raced ahead.

Probably going to get the seat next to Hart, Madison thought, hanging back a little bit. Once the enemy, always the enemy?

In her heart, she secretly wished that maybe she and Ivy could make time for some real understanding between each other. Of course, that would take some kind of holiday miracle, and Madison needed to reserve miracles for something more important, like Mom and Dad. She'd need a miracle to get them to stop fighting.

When Madison arrived home, Mom was on the phone, so she couldn't tell her about The Estates right away. Mom pointed to a note on the kitchen table: *Aimee called about tomorrow. Call back.*

Madison crumpled up the note and headed upstairs to change out of her clothes *and* pick out an outfit for the next day. She, Aimee, and Fiona were going to the hockey game together and that was a place to see and be seen. Madison guessed that was the reason for Aimee's call. She always wanted to compare clothes before big events.

As soon as Mom was off the phone, Madison dialed Aimee's house.

"Maddie! What's up?" Aimee said, breathlessly. She'd been practicing ballet in her basement. Her Dad had constructed a wooden floor and attached a small barre for her along one wall.

"You called *me*," Madison said. "What's up?"

"Oh. Yeah. I called," Aimee said. "Well . . . the thing is . . . I can't hang out tomorrow morning."

"You mean for the hockey game?" Madison asked. "But we—"

"No, no," Aimee said. "Before the hockey game. Something came up. Okay? I'll meet you later on at the rink."

"But we—" Madison started to say. "What came up?"

"Oh, Maddie, I have to go. Dean wants to use the phone," Aimee said. "Sorry. See you later? Bye!"

"But, Aim—" Madison started to say.

It was too late. Aimee had hung up the phone already.

Madison sat staring at the receiver as though she'd been hit by a rock.

48

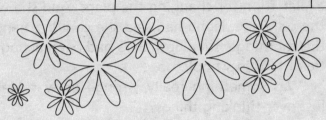

Madison's eyes traced a crack on her bedroom ceiling—down the wall, around her closet-door frame, and all the way to the floor. She snuggled under three quilts, digging her toes into the sheets to keep warm. Winter Saturday mornings in bed were the best: no rushing to school, walking the dog, or *anything*. Madison could just sleep and snuggle with Phinnie.

Especially since she wasn't getting together with Aimee this morning as she'd hoped. Last night's phone call had put those plans to rest.

Was it snowing today? Madison leaned out from under the covers to glance out the window. But there was no snow—just a blanket of gray sky. She began to wonder if it would *ever* snow this winter. Her windows weren't even that frosty this morning.

As Madison's eyes drifted back to the crack in the ceiling, she thought about her friends. It bugged Madison that Aimee didn't even really give a proper explanation for changing the plans. And she wasn't the only one. Fiona had said she couldn't hang out this morning either. Both BFFs had been acting a little distant in school, too.

Was something really wrong—or was Madison just over-thinking things?

Since her computer was still plugged into the spare phone jack in her bedroom from the night before, Madison grabbed it and crawled back into bed. Almost as good as snuggling in bed with Phin was snuggling in bed with her laptop.

She tried to push negative thoughts out of her mind as she opened her e-mailbox.

FROM	SUBJECT
✉ GoGramma	Re: Missing You
✉ GoGramma	Re: Missing You
✉ GoGramma	Re: Missing You
✉ Bigwheels	RE: Ski Trip

Three messages from Gramma? Madison laughed to herself. Sometimes, Gramma hit the SEND key too many times. Madison double-clicked one message to open it and deleted the other two.

From: GoGramma
To: MadFinn
Subject: Re: Missing You
Date: Fri 7 Dec 8:11 PM
_____

My dear Maddie, I am so very proud
of you! Of course I'm happy about
your volunteering. You are giving
so much. Your new grandmother must
be thrilled to have you as an
adopt-a-granddaughter. I know I am
happy to call you mine.

What is her name? Does she know how
lucky she is to have you visiting
with her? Remember that you always
get what you give.

You and your mother were right
about the telephone. My neighbor
Mabel helped me figure out what was
wrong. Time to get a new one.

I love you and think of you often.

Love,

Gramma Helen

After saving the Gramma message into her
"Gramma" file (where she saved most of the messages her grandmother ever sent), Madison opened

the message from Bigwheels. It was a long one with attachments.

From: Bigwheels
To: MadFinn
Subject: Re: Ski Trip
Date: Fri 7 Dec 11:11 PM

You have a lot going on right now, don'tcha? Me too. Winter is busy. Well, every time is busy, I guess. In answer to your question, ur right about the holidays being worse. It's so strange that u asked about my Mom & Dad fighting b/c lately they have been fighting A LOT again. My little brother Eddie has been sick with a cold and my little sister Melanie 2. I guess Mom needs a vacation. Well, that's what she says when she doesn't realize that I'm eavesdropping on them. I wish my parents would just make up their minds and be 2gether or not.

So I don't really have any advice for you about what to do when they argue except 1 main thing: don't EVER pick sides. Last week I was on my Dad's side about something and my mother got all mad at me and started crying. Actually, don't lie

to them either. Parents always know
or find out when u lie or cover up
stuff and then it is SO much worse.

Does that help? Are you singing
in the chorus or do you have a
solo for that winter concert? U
didn't say.

Write back soon.

Yours till the ice skates,

Bigwheels

P.S. I attached some poems to this
e-mail for u 2 read let me know if
u like them. One is from English
class.

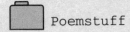 Poemstuff

Madison read Bigwheels e-mail through twice
and opened the poem file that had been attached.
She read through poems called "Snow Day," "Turkey
Sandwiches," "My Friendship," and "Listen Up."
They were all similar. Bigwheels wrote a lot about
finding true love and about friends. Madison liked
the poem "Hard to Find" the best. It was an alpha-
bet poem—at least up to the letter T.

Hard to Find

Always keep friends
Because they should be
Close by
Don't forget
Everyone needs them
Friendship is so important
Gives you a good feeling
Hard to find
I know it
Just find it
Kind
Loving friends
Make you feel good about you
Never critical
Open hearts
Putting you first
Quiet
Real
Special friends for special times
Take care of friends

Madison shot back an e-mail thanking Bigwheels for the advice and the poems. Then she tried to call Aimee again, to find out where they would be meeting at the hockey rink, but Aimee wasn't home. Neither was Fiona. When Madison called the Waterses' house, Fiona's twin brother Chet answered the phone and made some joke about his sister not being there.

Where were they?

Madison wondered if her BFFs were together—wherever they were.

After writing in her files and cleaning out part of her closet, Madison watched TV and helped Mom make date-nut bread. Lately, Mom had been into baking cookies and cakes and breads. Their entire cupboard was filled with treats. Before long, the afternoon arrived and Madison got dressed for the hockey game.

Since she still had not heard from Aimee or Fiona, Madison asked Mom to give her a ride over to the ice rink. She hoped her BFFs would be waiting there for Madison to arrive.

The rink was packed. Parents dropped off their kids out front. Mom pulled the car up to the curb to unload and Madison jumped out.

"I will pick you up in two hours," Mom said. "Play nice, okay?"

"Very funny, Mom," Madison said. She straightened out her ponytail and reknotted her striped scarf. Cold air nipped at her neck.

At first, Madison didn't see anyone she knew. But then, through a cluster of kids, Ivy came into view. She was standing by a door to the rink with Rose and Joanie. Madison walked over.

"Hey, Ivy," Madison said.

Rose turned and sneered. "Um . . . did you say something?" she asked.

Joanie laughed. "I think someone said something."

"I just said *hello*," Madison said. "And I said it to Ivy, not you."

"Well excuse me for living," Rose said. "Ivy, she said hello."

"Hi," Ivy said quietly, shooting a look at Rose.

"Can we please go in?" Joanie said, whining.

Madison couldn't believe it when they all three turned their backs to her and walked inside. Ivy was acting like a different person. The Ivy from The Estates trip the day before had been "Imposter Ivy." This was the more familiar attitude Madison knew from school.

Madison followed the enemy inside and approached the risers where everyone was sitting to watch the hockey game. She scanned the rows, searching for her friends. On one side of the seats were the Far Hills fans; and on the other side were fans from the opposing team, the Flames. Madison spotted Aimee and Fiona, talking together.

"Hey, you guys," Madison said, climbing over a few other kids to get to them. "I thought maybe you'd wait outside for me. What's up?"

Aimee and Fiona stopped whispering and turned to look at Madison.

"Oh my God, Maddie!" Aimee cried. "We totally saved you a seat."

Unfortunately, when Aimee turned around,

someone else had sat down there. They wouldn't move, so Madison sat in the row behind her friends.

"Hey, did you see Egg in his hockey gear?" Fiona asked. "He looks super-cute today!"

"You have Egg on the brain," Aimee said.

Fiona giggled. "Yeah, I guess so."

"So, Maddie," Aimee asked, twisting her body around. "What did you do today?"

"Hung out," Madison replied. "Alone," she added.

"Look, I'm sorry about canceling our plans today but we both had other really important stuff to do that I forgot about," Aimee explained. "Right, Fiona?"

"Yeah, plans," Fiona said. "Really important plans."

"Huh? Where were you guys?" Madison asked.

Just then, the bullhorn sounded. The game was about to begin. Since it was just a junior-high scrimmage, there weren't very many spectators, but everyone was screaming at the top of their lungs. Madison could no longer hear a word Aimee or Fiona said.

The players skated out onto the ice with sticks in the air. Egg did look kind of sweet in his hockey gear. He was playing goalie. Drew Maxwell, one of Egg's best pals, was in the right wing position. He was fast. Hart skated quickly around the ice, too. Madison's eyes followed him. She'd heard that he'd won awards for skating. Bigwheels would be impressed.

Madison's keypal loved ice skating more than any-thing, even if it was only hockey players, not figure skaters, doing it.

As the game began, Fiona and Aimee tried turn-ing around to talk, but it was so hard to hear that they'd turn right back around again. Even though Madison was in the middle of the crowd, she felt a little alone sitting there. Ivy and her drones were all the way down toward the front, right near the ice. Madison guessed that Ivy was probably making eyes at Hart through the barrier. Poison Ivy would do any-thing to be closer to him.

Kids spun loud noisemakers and yelled for their favorite players on both sides. When Egg made a big save with his glove, Fiona jumped up and clapped. Madison wanted to do the same when Hart scored a goal, but she restrained herself. Liking him was her biggest secret; and she'd do anything to protect it.

The game got boring after a while, so Madison decided to go to the bathroom. On the way out, she nearly collided with an old woman who smiled and went on her way. Madison thought of Mrs. Romano and wondered what her adoptive grandmother was doing at The Estates while she was here watching hockey. Did she have grandchildren who played hockey? Did she have any family? Madison realized that during their visit she'd forgotten to ask some important questions.

From inside the bathroom, Madison heard the

crowd roar. She guessed that the Far Hills team had gotten another goal and hurried to get back to her seat. The scrimmage lasted for another half an hour, and then everyone filed out of the ice rink. Madison still had twenty minutes to wait for Mom, so she asked Aimee and Fiona to wait with her.

"Well," Fiona said. "Actually, we can't really wait because my dad is coming to pick us up. . . ."

"Yeah," Aimee interrupted, "but . . . do you need a ride?"

"Well, my mom is coming back," Madison said.

"Oh," Fiona said. "So you don't need a ride?"

"I guess not," Madison said.

"Well, we can all talk later," Aimee said.

"Later?" Madison said. She felt a twinge in the pit of her stomach, like something was very wrong.

"Yeah, later. I'll e-mail you," Aimee said. "For sure."

"Look, there's my dad's car," Fiona yelled. Mr. Waters waved from the car. Madison waved back.

Everyone stood around staring at each other.

"Are you guys mad at me or something?" Madison asked.

Aimee and Fiona looked at each other but didn't say anything.

Madison sighed. "Because I feel a little out of it. You guys couldn't hang out earlier today and you were barely talking to me during the game and . . ."

"Oh my God! Mad at you? NO WAY!" Aimee squealed. She leaned in to give Madison a huge hug.

59

Fiona joined in for a three-way hug. "We're SO not mad, Maddie."

"Oh my God, why would you *ever* think we were mad?" Aimee asked.

"I don't know," Madison said, more confused than before.

Mr. Waters honked the horn.

"We have to go now," Fiona said.

"I know, I know," Madison said. "E me later, right?"

"Of course!" Aimee and Flona both cried.

The pair piled into Mr. Waters's car, and it disappeared through the rink parking lot's exit gate. By now, the rest of the seventh graders began to disappear, too. Hart, Drew, and Egg got into the car to drive home together with Señora Diaz. Ivy came out and she and the drones got into Mr. Daly's car. Ivy even waved good-bye when she left.

Madison leaned up against a wall and waited for Mom.

Luckily, Mom arrived on the scene a few moments later.

"How was the game?" she asked as Madison got into the front seat.

"Okay, I guess," Madison replied. "We won. But I feel like I'm on another planet."

Mom fished around for more details, but Madison didn't know how to explain. She didn't have the words yet. When they got back home, however, Madison went upstairs immediately, opened a new file, and started to write.

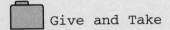 Give and Take

Major newsflash: Ivy the enemy is being friendly (well, sometimes) and Aimee and Fiona the friends are acting like the enemy (avoiding me?).

Repeat after me: HUH???

Okay, so my BFFs aren't really being mean or n e thing, but I get this strange feeling that they don't want to hang out together. That hurts me a little. What's worse is when they get all nice with me, which is especially unlike Aimee. She only does that when she's acting fake. I've never seen her do that to anyone but people she doesn't like. Why would she have to be fake with ME?

I am so confused. How am I supposed to celebrate the holidays when my BFFs don't want to even ride home with me and my mom and dad won't stop fighting? I hope that things get better in time for the Winter Jubilee concert. We have a lot of singing rehearsals coming up.

Gramma Helen says that I'll get what I give. Just when does that start, exactly? I thought I was giving a lot.

Rude Awakening: It's hard to have a warm heart, when all I'm getting is the cold shoulder.

Chapter 6

By Monday morning, everything seemed to be back to normal with Aimee and Fiona. They called and e-mailed when they said they would over the weekend. Aimee even came by with Blossom to walk Phin together. Neither girl explained why she had acted so strangely at the hockey game, but Madison didn't require an explanation. She just wanted her old BFFs back.

Not everyone was back to their normal selves, however. Ivy was as fake as ever, pasting on her super-grin Monday afternoon when they drove to The Estates for the second official visit. She sat near Madison again—not Hart.

"I have been missing Mrs. Wood all weekend," Ivy said as they boarded the minibus.

"Missing her? But you only just met her," Madison said.

"Well, you know," Ivy said with a dramatic flourish, waving her arm in the air. "I get very attached to people quickly."

"You do?" Madison said, stifling a giggle.

"Sure I do," Ivy said.

And you get unattached pretty quickly, too, Madison thought.

"Don't you care about *your* person?" Ivy asked.

"You make it sound so funny," Madison said. "Like we have them on loan from the library or something."

"Well, Nurse Ana and Mr. Lynch said we are responsible for them," Ivy said.

Madison smiled. "Yeah, for like an hour. Ivy, you are so . . ."

"So . . . what? I am taking my responsibility very seriously," Ivy said. Madison could almost hear the old, familiar snarl in Ivy's voice.

"I've thought about Mrs. Romano a lot," Madison said. "She and I had fun talking on Friday. I just think she's lonely."

"I would be lonely, too, if I lived there," Ivy said. "Mrs. Wood doesn't act lonely at all."

"That's not what I mean," Madison said. "Mrs. Romano seems lonely because she has no real friends. Well, except her birds."

"Her birds?" Ivy asked.

"She watches them from the windows," Madison explained.

63

"What a freak," Ivy said.

Madison frowned. "Sometimes you can be so . . . so . . ."

"What?" Ivy asked. "So . . . what?"

"RUDE," Madison blurted. "I can't believe you're even volunteering. Why do you bother?"

Ivy got very quiet, which surprised Madison. Normally, Poison Ivy would snap back with some obnoxious comment of her own, but she didn't say anything at all. She just shrunk down into her gray wool coat and sulked. Madison actually started to feel a little guilty about what she'd said.

When they arrived, Nurse Ana was there to greet the seventh graders. "*Hola!*" she cried as the electric swinging doors to The Estates opened up.

Everyone filed into the conference room. Each visit required a reorientation with the social director. Davy Miller was bummed out because there were no sodas this time.

"Did everyone have a good weekend?" Mr. Lynch asked.

Señora Diaz told the kids to talk about any concerns or questions they had after the first visit, but of course no one had any. Everyone just sat around and stared. Joey O'Neill picked his nose, and ate it too, this time.

When they were finally "dismissed" to go meet their adoptive grandparents in the rooms, Ivy pulled Madison aside.

"Look," she said seriously. "I'm sorry about what I said on the bus, okay?"

"You are?" Madison asked with disbelief.

"I bet your fake grandmother is really nice," Ivy said. "I only said what I said because . . . well, just forget it."

"Yeah, I will," Madison said.

"And don't tell anyone what I said, okay?"

"Okay."

Madison promised it would be their secret. She hadn't had a secret with Ivy since third grade.

"See you later on the bus," Ivy said as she walked away.

Madison nodded and headed off in the direction of Mrs. Romano's room.

Along the way, she peered into the rooms that had standard linoleum tile floors. Some had art on the walls, bookcases, and bureaus. Others had bare walls and plain wood furniture that Madison guessed belonged to The Estates.

The residents themselves were strolling through the halls or eating late lunches from rolling trays in their rooms. Madison saw a pair of older women dressed in sweatpants and T-shirts. They said hello and told her they were heading off to Seniors Yoga class. Madison laughed at that. She imagined that if Gramma Helen lived here one day that was exactly what she might be doing.

Some of the people walking around didn't look

as happy as Mrs. Holly Wood or other residents. An older man coughed his way past her, pushing his walker inch by inch. Another woman growled at Madison for getting in her way.

Madison finally reached Mrs. Romano's room and found her adopt-a-grandmother lying across the bed.

"I've been expecting you," Mrs. Romano said. "I'm glad you're back."

"Of course I'm back," Madison said. "How are you?"

"Tired," Mrs. Romano said. "My medication makes me tired sometimes. I just need to stay still. Sometimes it's the weather that does me in. My aching bones say it's going to snow soon."

"I hope so," Madison said. "I want to go skiing."

"You ski?" Mrs. Romano said, laughing. "I bet you fly down the mountain."

Madison smiled. "Well, not exactly. I'm just a beginner."

"Well, someday you'll fly," Mrs. Romano said.

"Like your birds," Madison said.

Mrs. Romano laughed again. "Oh yes!"

"Have you been watching them today?" Madison asked.

"There were a few cardinals out this morning. But the cold keeps some of them away, I think."

"You should have a bird feeder," Madison said.

"I suppose so," Mrs. Romano said. "But they don't let us do anything special around here. Except have special visitors." She winked.

Madison sat down in the chair near Mrs. Romano's bed and they talked more about the birds. Fifteen minutes into their conversation, Madison finally got the nerve to ask personal questions about family. Who was the real Mrs. Romano and what was her life like before she moved into The Estates? Madison sounded like a news reporter.

Mrs. Romano dove *way* back into her memory banks. She began to reminisce about her girlhood. She had been born in Canada on an island where her father and grandfather were fishermen. Her mother was the lighthouse keeper. One sister had died when Mrs. Romano was younger, but she had a brother who lived in Europe. Her love for birds had started when a young boy she liked once gave her a parakeet as a present.

Madison glanced over and saw the photo of the parakeet on the wall.

"His name was Wally," Mrs. Romano explained. "Like my beau."

Madison liked the word *beau* instead of *boyfriend*. She wondered what it would sound like to say that Hart was *her* beau.

"Did you get married?" Madison asked.

Mrs. Romano shook her head. "Never found the time," she laughed.

"I think it's nice that you have so many bird friends," Madison said. "At least they can't get all weird on you . . . like my friends do."

"I'm sure your friends aren't getting weird on purpose," Mrs. Romano said.

"Sometimes I feel like I'm watching my life happen from the outside looking in," Madison explained. "But I guess I'll just get over it."

As Madison explained the whole story, Mrs. Romano bowed her head down.

"Go over to my dresser," Mrs. Romano said from her perch on the bed. "Get me that snow globe on top there. I want to tell you a story."

Madison walked over to find the small globe amid a pile of silk scarves.

"Now, take it in your hand and shake it," Mrs. Romano instructed.

Madison lifted the globe into the air and shook hard. Inside the plastic, a miniature snowman danced under a glittering snowfall. He had a black hat and green scarf, stick arms, and a carrot nose. The snow inside the globe sparkled.

"Once upon a time," Mrs. Romano explained, "my best friend gave that globe to me. Every winter, she and I would build a snowman together. No matter where we were, we'd make time to get together and build one. She flew all the way from London, England, to make a snowman with me one year. But then another year she called to say that she had the flu and she couldn't meet with me. She sent this instead: the perfect snowman inside that globe."

"What a cool story," Madison said.

"That was the last snowman we ever built," Mrs. Romano explained.

"Last?" Madison cried. "What happened?"

"The flu turned out to be pneumonia. Yes, it was very sad. But I didn't tell you the story to make you sad," Mrs. Romano said.

Madison felt tears in her own eyes. "You didn't?" she sniffled.

"You should always tell your friends what's really on your mind. Don't waste a moment. What's given to us can be taken away just like *that,* and we need to treasure it."

"Wow," Madison said. "That's something Gramma Helen would say."

"Come sit by me," Mrs. Romano said. "When you visited last week, I was so grouchy. But you made me happy. I wanted you to know that."

"You're welcome," Madison said.

"Sometimes I'm not myself," Mrs. Romano said. "Well, that's what Nurse Ana and some of the other aides tell me. And I don't have many visitors these days. I have early Alzheimer's disease. They did tell you that, didn't they?"

Madison nodded. "I'm not really sure what it is though."

"Sometimes I forget things," she explained. "Once I forgot my own name and I wandered off down the street. Don't ask how I got off the property! I don't even know. But that only happened once so far. I'm afraid it will happen more often as I get older."

"That sounds really sad," Madison said.

"Oh listen to me, complaining!" Mrs. Romano said. "You've done nothing but keep me company, and I tell you depressing stories. Shame on me! I'm fine now. Let's talk about happy things. Tell me more about your friends."

Madison laughed. "I'm so lucky I got paired with you. You are so smart. Can I ask you something?"

Mrs. Romano nodded. "Of course. You can ask me anything you want. This adopt-a-grandmother thing goes both ways. You give to me and I give back."

Madison began to babble even more—about her parents this time.

"So mom and dad got divorced and this Christmas they're acting so angry about everything. They both want me to spend the holidays with them as usual, but of course I can't be in two places at once. What am I supposed to do if they're fighting a lot? I know you don't know them or anything, but they always seem to put me right in the middle of their problems and you seem to know so much—"

Mrs. Romano held up her hand. "Hold it right there," she said. "About your parents: here's what I think. Sometimes when people love you so much they get all worked up about it. They both want you to be with them. That's understandable."

"So what am I supposed to do?" Madison asked.

"Tell them how you feel. Be yourself," Mrs. Romano said.

"That's it?" Madison asked.

"Being in the middle is great if you're in a hug," Mrs. Romano said. "Otherwise it's for the birds."

They both laughed and looked over at the wall with all the bird pictures.

Later that night back at home, Madison hooked up her laptop in the kitchen. That way, she could type *and* keep Mom company while Mom made dinner.

Of course, Madison ended up writing in her files way more than chopping vegetables.

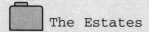 The Estates

On the bus home from The Estates today, Ivy was acting all shmoozy again. I just don't get it. She's like a totally different person all of a sudden. Of course, she's still the same old evil Poison Ivy at school.

Mrs. Romano is way cool. She told me that if Ivy is behaving like two different people then she's probably just insecure. Could that be true? Ivy? Mrs. Romano also has an answer for everything. She even loaned me this very cool matched hat and scarf set that she knit a long time ago. It has an orange pom-pom on top—can you

71

believe that? My favorite color in the world!

I am so glad that I volunteered at The Estates. It is nice to know that not everyone is acting bizarre around the holidays. Mrs. Romano may be the one who is supposedly sick but she's making more sense to me these days than Mom or Dad or my BFFs.

"Maddie," Mom asked. "Would you keep an eye on this boiling pot while I go make a quick phone call?"

Madison nodded and opened up her e-mailbox. She'd watch the pot out of the corner of her eye, but she had something more important to do first. She had someone she needed to say something to—right at that exact moment.

It couldn't wait.

From: MadFinn
To: GoGramma
Subject: Guess what?
Date: Mon 10 Dec 5:53 PM

I love you. Thanks for being such a nice grandmother. I was thinking about you today a lot. I don't tell you that enough.

xoxxo

Maddie

After she hit SEND, she searched for Bigwheels online, but her keypal was nowhere to be found. But surprisingly, Madison did find Aimee and Fiona. They were in an online chat room together. Madison considered jumping into their chat, or even just observing them. . . .

"Maddie!" Mom screeched from behind the kitchen table.

Madison turned to see Mom frantically wiping off the stove and floor. The pot had boiled over.

"Didn't I ask you to watch this for me?" Mom asked. "Thank goodness I was only boiling potatoes."

"Whoops," Madison said. "Sorry, Mom."

Mom sighed and turned down the burner, bringing her pot to a slower simmer. "Next time, please pay better attention?" Mom pleaded. "That computer can be such a distraction sometimes."

Madison waited for Mom to exit the kitchen once more before pulling up the Web site again. She checked bigfishbowl.com for the chat room with Aimee and Fiona, but it was empty. Neither BFF was online anymore.

Dejected, Madison logged off and shut down the laptop.

Why hadn't her friends Insta-messaged her? Didn't they check to see if Madison was online at the same time? Why were they acting exclusive online with each other and *without* her?

Maybe it was better NOT to know.

Chapter 7

On Tuesday morning, Madison started getting more worried about her BFFs again. In between classes, Madison saw Aimee and Fiona in the midst of a private conversation. But when she walked up to join them, the talking stopped.

Stopped.

It wasn't the sort of holiday spirit Madison expected from her closest girlfriends—or anyone else.

During lunch period, Madison spotted Aimee again down in the cafeteria, but without Fiona this time.

"Aimee?" Madison asked as she got on line for macaroni and cheese.

"Hi, Maddie! Hey, did you try their homemade granola? It's actually good," Aimee said, sliding a banana and yogurt onto her lunch tray.

"Aimee, can I ask you something?" Madison said.

Aimee turned around. "Is something wrong?"

"You tell me," Madison said.

"Huh?" Aimee asked.

"Is something wrong?" Madison asked.

"Wrong?" Aimee repeated. She smiled knowingly. "Oh, I get it. You're still freaked about the other day at the ice rink. You know that when Fiona and I got that ride home from the hockey game you *totally* could have come along. You know that, right?"

"I know," Madison said. "But there's other stuff going on. I feel like I'm . . . well, in the way when I'm around you and Fiona."

"In the way?" Aimee tugged at her braid. "Maddie, what are you talking about?"

From the way Aimee twisted and pulled at her hair, Madison knew she was making her BFF uncomfortable.

"I can't believe you would think that," Aimee said.

"So I'm not in the way?" Madison said, looking for further reassurance.

"Of course not. Hey, I'm starved," Aimee said. "Can we talk about this at the table?"

Madison shrugged as Gilda Z the lunch lady scooped a ladle of macaroni and cheese onto her plate. Hopefully, it tastes better than it looks, Madison thought, because it looks like radioactive yellow glop.

After Aimee and Madison got their drinks, they headed toward their usual orange table at the back of the room.

"I'll catch up with you, Aim," Madison called out. "I just have to ask Ivy something."

Aimee made a face and kept walking. Madison approached the yellow lunch table at the center of the cafeteria. This was Ivy and the drones' regular dining spot.

"Hey, Ivy," Madison said, shifting from foot to foot. "Did you write up that essay about The Estates?"

Señora Diaz had asked all the volunteers to write up a profile of their recent visit, including details about the resident's family, likes, and dislikes.

Ivy looked up but didn't say anything right away.

"I was thinking maybe we could write ours together," Madison suggested.

Rose Thorn grunted. "I'm sorry, Madison. Did you say what I think you said?"

"Yeah," Joanie repeated. "Did you just ask—?"

"I was talking to Ivy," Madison snapped, rolling her eyes.

"Well she's not talking to you, I guess," Joanie said, laughing to herself.

"No, I haven't written mine yet," Ivy said at last, giving Rose and Joan a hard look. "But I don't really think we should work on ours together."

"Of course you shouldn't," Joanie blurted.

"Fine," Madison said, feeling like she'd been chopped off at the knees.

"Um . . . is there something else we can help you with?" Rose asked.

"I guess not," Madison said, staring at Ivy.

"Why did you volunteer for The Estates anyhow?" Joanie asked. "A bunch of old people? What a party!"

Rose chuckled. "The real reason you're doing it, Ivy, is because Hart's doing it, too. Right?"

Ivy kicked Rose under the table. "Why don't you just zip it?" she said in a commanding tone.

"He's such a hottie, though," Joanie said. "I don't blame you."

Madison wanted to hit Joan the drone on the side of the head with the lunch tray and run far, far away. Not only because Joan was being obnoxious, but also because she'd called attention to the truth about Hart—a truth Madison hated to acknowledge.

Ivy was after Hart, too. No matter how nice Ivy could be in the outside world, in the lunchroom she was still enemy number one—even when it came to boys. Madison had to keep reminding herself of that fact.

So instead of pulling a hit-and-run, Madison stood her ground. "Well, thanks anyway," she said. "See you later, Ivy?"

"See you later, Ivy?" Rose teased, mocking Madison's tone.

Madison shrugged. "Whatever." She turned to walk away, but nearly tripped over her own shoelaces.

"Whoops. Don't fall now," Joanie said, cracking up.

Luckily, Madison kept her balance. She bent down to retie her shoe, placing her tray on the floor.

"How embarrassing," Joanie whispered loudly.

Madison could hear every word. She stood up. "Embarrassing?" she said with a snarl.

"I know Ivy volunteers," Joanie said, ignoring Madison. "But you're the class president. You have to do those things. What's Madison's excuse?"

"Yeah, and you'd rather hang out with us after school anyway, right, Ivy?" Rose said.

"Who really wants to visit a bunch of old people?" Joanie quipped.

Madison raised her tray up, ready to hurl macaroni and cheese into their faces. But she didn't. She walked away at last—anger swelling inside her chest like a balloon that wanted to POP.

How could Ivy just sit there and let them say those things? Madison fumed. What happened to Mrs. Holly Wood and the fun times Ivy had during their visits? Now Ivy was letting the drones make jokes about the nursing home? Ivy was the queen of their little clique. Why didn't she butt in and tell Rose and Joanie to just SHUT UP?

By the time Madison reached the orange table at

the back of the room, she was all worked up. Egg was holding court telling some pathetic joke about a dead skunk.

"Eeeeuw! That really smells!" Drew joked back after Egg revealed the not-so-funny punch line.

Fiona, who had finally arrived, was seated near the boys, just across the lunch table from Aimee. As soon as Madison approached, she saw Fiona whisper to Aimee and slip a notebook into her book bag.

More secrets?

Madison was too angry about Ivy to care. She walked up to the table and gasped. "I can't believe what just happened," Madison said.

"Did you tell off the drones?" Aimee asked, grinning. "That Rose is such a cow. I know you let her have it. Dish!"

"I didn't really let anyone have it," Madison said with a sigh. "Not exactly."

"Wait! Tell us what happened," Fiona sajd.

Madison slid between Aimee and Drew. Hart was all the way down the other end of the table.

"They were making fun of volunteering," Madison said.

"Gosh," Aimee said sarcastically. "Making fun? Now, that's a big surprise."

"It was mostly the drones. Ivy didn't say much," Madison admitted, plowing her fork through watery macaroni and gulping chocolate milk. "But still . . ."

"What were you stopping to talk to Ivy about

anyway?" Fiona asked. "I thought you didn't speak to the enemy, especially at lunch."

Madison groaned. "I was just asking Ivy about this assignment we have about The Estates."

"Why not ask Egg?" Aimee asked.

Madison shrugged. "I don't know. I was talking to Ivy about it on the bus the other day and—"

"You're spending a lot of time at The Estates, aren't you?" Fiona asked.

"How's the lady you see there? What did you call her?" Aimee asked.

"Her name is Eleanor Romano. Some people call her the Bird Lady," Madison explained.

"Bird lady?" Fiona said. "That sounds fun."

"NO ONE is as much fun as Smokey!" Egg cried, eavesdropping and interrupting.

Madison laughed and explained to Aimee and Fiona. "Smokey is this man that Egg sees on his visits. He wears tie-dye shirts. Brags about his ten great-grandkids. Talks about World War II a lot, too."

"Uh . . . is Smokey all covered with snow?" Drew yelled out, singing some more of the song.

Egg punched Drew in the shoulder. "Nice one, Drew boy," he said. "Believe it or not, Smokey is ninety-one. He was just telling me that he climbed Mount Everest once and he skydived with his son until he was in his seventies. Plus, he's a veteran of two wars."

"Wow," some other boys at the table said.

"Who does Ivy visit?" Fiona asked.

Madison rolled her eyes. "Someone perfect, just like her. Of course."

"HA!" Aimee cackled. "Good one, Maddie."

Madison put down her fork. "I wonder why Ivy even volunteers. Does she really care, deep down? I just heard her making fun of the people who live at The Estates."

"What did she say?" Fiona asked.

"It's more like what *didn't* she say," Madison said. "She let Rose and Joanie say the meanest things— and didn't tell them to be quiet."

"Maybe she agrees with them," Aimee said with a mouthful of granola. "She's a good actress, don't forget. And she's queen of the Fakers."

"Yeah," Madison said glumly, glancing back over at Ivy's table. It was getting harder than hard to distinguish between her enemy's many moods.

"Don't kill me for saying this, but I don't think Ivy is so evil all the time," Fiona said, taking a bit of her salad. "She's actually okay when she's not around the drones."

Madison nodded. "Yeah, I guess she is different when Rose and Joanie aren't around."

"What are you saying? Poison Ivy isn't so bad? Maddie, you hate her!" Aimee said.

"I don't really 'hate' anyone. Do I?" Madison asked. "Don't worry, Aim. It's not like I'm not starting an Ivy fan club or anything."

A voice came over the loudspeaker. Kids participating in the holiday poinsettia sale were asked to meet up in the greenhouse.

"Aim, we have to go," Fiona blurted. She looked across at Madison. "Sorry. Aimee and I have to go."

"Where?" Madison asked. "You're not selling plants, are you?"

"Um . . . no . . . we have to go to the . . . darkroom . . ." Fiona said.

Aimee elbowed Fiona in the ribs. "She meant we have to meet with a teacher," Aimee recovered.

"Meet a teacher in the darkroom?" Madison asked, cracking a smile. "Who? Principal Bernard?"

Fiona and Aimee laughed. "Very funny, Maddie," they said at practically the same time.

"No, seriously. You're leaving me in the lunchroom alone?" Madison said, tapping her fork on the table.

"You're not alone. There are like fifty other people here," Aimee said.

"E me later?" Madison asked. She wouldn't see either of her BFFs for the rest of the day. They didn't have any afternoon classes together.

"I'll be home from ballet late," Aimee said. "I'll try to e-mail or call when I get home."

"Me, too," Fiona said, picking up her books. "After soccer."

Madison watched Aimee and Fiona rush off together. Since Drew and the rest of the boys at the table were engrossed in a boring conversation about race cars, Madison had no one left to talk to. She tried to eat more of her macaroni, but it had cooled. She hoped that dinner with Dad would be a better and happier meal.

Across the room, Ivy, Rose, and Joanie got up from their table and headed toward the exit doors located directly behind the orange table where Madison was sitting. Madison put down her head and pretended to be playing with her macaroni so she wouldn't have to face any more of their snide remarks.

"See you later, Madison," Ivy said as she walked by.

Rose and Joanie tittered.

"Later," Madison said, nodding in Ivy's direction.

Ivy nodded back and followed the drones out of the room. It looked odd to see them file away in reverse order. Usually, Ivy was the one leading follow-the-leader, but not today.

For a moment, everything about friendships at Far Hills seemed flipped around.

Madison wondered how long the weirdness could last.

French Toast, the restaurant Dad picked for Tuesday night's dinner, was slower than slow. It took the waiter ten minutes to come over with any menus. When Dad asked for a second glass of water, he had to ask two people for refills before anyone even considered pouring one.

The decor was holiday tacky, too, Madison laughed to herself. They had a collection of stuffed Santas and bears in Santa caps all along one wall; and multicolored lights across the mantel of a stone fireplace. The air smelled like pine needle potpourri, sticky-sweet and burnt at the same time.

Somehow, in spite of the decorations (and smells) in the dining room, Madison was not feeling holiday spirited. Dad had canceled their dream ski vacation. How could she be feeling good about that—or anything else?

"I hear they have delicious food here," Dad said, reading his menu. "I'm getting some calamari. Who wants to share?"

"Whatever," Madison mumbled, reading hers. "I think I'm going to have a hamburger."

"Here?" Dad said. "But this is fine food, Maddie. Don't you want a pork chop or fish or a steak?"

"Dad . . ." Madison moaned.

"Fine, get whatever you want. I won't tell you what to eat," Dad said.

"Fine," Madison said gruffly.

"Are you still mad at me about that ski trip?" Dad asked.

Madison looked over at him. "Not exactly *mad*, Dad. I love being stuck inside doing nothing for my whole winter vacation."

"Maddie, don't be that way. Besides, we can reschedule the ski trip for another time," Dad urged.

"Like when?" Madison asked. "Next Christmas?"

"Well, I have a business trip next week," Dad said. He pulled out his electronic organizer. "So that means we can get together . . ."

"Work, work, work," Madison chanted. "Blah, blah, blah."

"We have had this conversation before," Dad said. He put away the calendar. "Okay, let's switch gears. Let's talk about you. Tell me about what's going on at school."

Madison told Dad about volunteering at The Estates. She described her visit with Eleanor Romano.

"Sounds like a nice woman," Dad said. The waiter brought over a basket of bread, and he grabbed a piece.

"But she has Alzheimer's disease," Madison explained. "At least that's what she said."

"Wow. Really?" Dad said. "And she talks about that with you? Did the doctors and nurses explain this to you?"

"Of course, Dad. They like to prepare us for anything that might happen during one of our visits, so we've talked honestly about stuff," Madison said. "Some residents are handicapped and one lady is deaf. Hilary, the girl who visits with her, speaks sign language."

"Alzheimer's is serious stuff," Dad said, taking a deep, deep breath. "You can't let it upset you though. Okay?"

"What do you know about it?" Madison asked.

Dad pushed himself away from the table and got very quiet.

"Dad?" Madison asked. "What's the matter?"

"I never told you this, Maddie, but my Dad, your Grampa Max, suffered from Alzheimer's disease. At least that's what the doctors suspected. He got sick very quickly."

"Grampa Max?" Madison said. She hardly ever heard about Dad's parents, because they had both died before Madison was born. Gramma Ruth had died years before Madison arrived, and Grampa Max had died only the week before. He just missed meeting his first—and only grandchild.

Dad's voice quivered as he described the way his father used to talk about his own boyhood. "He was a real spitfire, your grandfather," Dad said.

"Is it true that you named me after him?" Madison asked.

"Half true. Your mother was an assistant director at Budge Films at the time. She was working on a documentary about Dolly Madison. We both loved the name. And it seemed a good match, too—an *M* name, in memory of Grampa Max."

"Wow," Madison said, beaming. "I never heard that story before."

"Really?" Dad said.

"I really wish you would talk about your parents more, Dad," Madison said. "I wish I'd known them."

By now, the waiter had brought the appetizers to the table. Madison sunk a spoon into her French onion soup while Dad dipped his calamari into a bowl of red sauce.

"Oh, brother!" he cried, dropping the food. Sauce had dribbled all over the tablecloth and his shirt.

"We don't have to talk now if you don't want," Madison blurted, sensing that something was wrong.

"Yes we do," Dad said, wiping off the sauce and placing his hand on Madison's arm. "We have to talk. I don't know why we haven't talked before."

He moved his chair closer to Madison and started to describe Grampa Max's life.

Madison hung on Dad's every word.

Chapter 8

 What I Don't Know

Dad told me all this stuff about Grampa
Max last night. I can't stop thinking about
it. Grampa was in World War II, just like
Smokey. I didn't know that. I have to tell
Egg. And he flew planes, too. Isn't that
amazing? Dad also told me that Gramma Ruth
was a seamstress. How did I miss all that
information? I need to keep a file on my
family history.

Dad talked a lot about the past—even
about loving Mom, which seems like forever
ago. He gets all mushy when he talks about
her, which is the opposite of how she
talks. What am I supposed to say when he
does that? And as soon as I asked him about
their fighting (which is nonstop these
days) he denied it flat out. He told me I

shouldn't worry so much. Is he joking?

That's not the only joke. Poison Ivy is one, too. After everything that happened with the drones yesterday, I figured she would ignore me permanently. But today I saw her in the hall before second period and she said hello. Of course I saw her with Joanie later on this afternoon and she blew me off big time. Does Ivy have multiple personalities? Is she nicer when she's droneless?

But the worst joke of all is the weather. "Snow, snow, snow," says the weather lady with the big hair on the Weather Channel. Ha, ha, ha.

Rude Awakening: The only blizzard in Far Hills is inside my head. There is so much I don't know—and so much more that I don't get.

Madison hit SAVE and glanced at the clock in the school media lab. She had exactly ten minutes to pack up her stuff and get downstairs to the chorus room. Rehearsal for the Winter Jubilee was starting at three o'clock.

By the time Madison got to Mrs. Montefiore's classroom, everyone had taken up all the good seats. The band was down in front with flutes and clarinets and two kids at the piano. Madison spied Dan Ginsburg seated near the front, flute in hand. He waved to her.

She played the flute, too. But Madison only went

to lessons sometimes. Dan practiced almost every day. Seeing him sitting there made Madison wish she'd practiced more.

"Over here, Maddie!" Fiona yelled across the room.

"Over heeeeere!" her brother Chet said, imitating her. She promptly smacked him on the knee.

Madison laughed and made her way up the row toward Fiona, Aimee, Hart, Drew, and the rest of the gang. Thankfully, they'd saved Madison a seat. And it was in the middle of everyone, not such a bad place to be.

The band started its warm-up as more kids filed in. The teachers waited until the room was nearly packed before starting the vocal warm-ups.

Tap, tap, tap.

At three forty-five, Mrs. Montefiore tapped her music stand and asked the band to play some scales—finally.

Do, re, mi, fa, sol, la, ti, do.

It didn't matter if some kids were off-pitch, like Madison. This was all about the experience and the act of trying to help, and not about being a super-singer, right? That was what Madison hoped.

When Egg sang, every *ahhh* sounded like *quaaack*—like a duck.

Hart rubbed his hands together when he was trying to remember words.

Aimee bounced when she sang.

Madison glanced around. Fiona was the most exciting. Her voice sounded like a flute, the way she jumped from high note to low note and back up again. And a few rows away, someone else was singing just as beautifully.

Madison listened close, straining her neck to see.

It was Ivy Daly. And she knew she was good. Ivy was flipping her hair before every chorus of "Sleigh Ride." Madison watched her from behind.

"'Oh, it's lovely weather for a sleigh ride together with yoooooo,'" Hart sang loudly and poked Madison in the back until she jumped.

"'Giddyap, giddyap!'" Egg cracked.

"'Giddyap, let's go,'" Aimee trilled, bouncing her knees.

"'We're riding in a wonderland of snoooooooow,'" Fiona sang.

Mrs. Montefiore stopped the class at least three or four times so the kids could get the lyrics and notes right. But Madison was more interested in the singers and not the song. She kept her eyes glued to the enemy.

"Beautiful job!" Mrs. Montefiore exclaimed as soon as the band played the final note. "We've got a wonderful concert or two ahead of us."

The room buzzed with voices and energy—the holiday spirit Madison had in mind. Parents would love the concert at school. And the folks at The Estates would love theirs, too. Madison knew Mrs. Romano would be singing right along for sure.

Kids hushed up as Mrs. Montefiore blew a new note into her gold pitch pipe. She frantically waved her arm into the air to get everyone's attention for the start of the next song, "You're a Mean One, Mr. Grinch."

Madison snickered to herself. She remembered Fiona's words from the very first meeting for the Winter Jubilee: "The Grinch song should be dedicated to Ivy and her drones."

That was no joke.

"SNOW!" Madison screeched. "Look! Snow!" She held out her hand to catch a falling snowflake and watch crystals melt in her palm.

Aimee stuck out her tongue to taste it. "I wish this came in chocolate or butter crunch," she said.

"Look, it's the sticky kind," Fiona said, leaning over to touch the sidewalk with her brown, knit mittens.

The three friends walked home slowly from singing practice, evaluating the weather—and their fellow classmates—every step of the way.

"Rose Thorn fell in dance class today," Aimee said. "I started to laugh. We had visitors, and I didn't want to act rude. But it was hysterical."

"How can you laugh at someone when she's down?" Fiona asked.

"You sound like a self-help commercial!" Aimee said.

Madison grumbled. "Fiona, they laugh at us. Why can't we make fun of them, too?"

"Karma," Fiona explained. "You get what you give."

Madison gasped. "What did you say, Fiona?" It was what Gramma Helen always said to Madison.

"You get what you give, Maddie," Fiona repeated. "If you're mean to someone, then you'll get meanness in return. I totally believe that."

"Wow-weeee," Aimee joked.

"Quit making fun," Fiona said. "I'm a hundred percent serious."

"Soh-reeee," Aimee said, smiling.

Madison knew Fiona was righter than right. The same was true for Poison Ivy Daly. If Madison kept being mean to the enemy, then she'd only get meanness in return.

As the trio walked along, snow continued falling, but lightly. There was no storm on the way, not as far as Madison could see. This was just a dusting, in spite of what the big-haired weather lady said.

"Now that your trip was canceled, what are you doing for Christmas break?" Fiona asked Madison.

Madison shrugged. "I don't know. Maybe I'll spend some more time with Mrs. Romano at The Estates."

"And you're coming over to my house, too," Aimee cried.

Fiona giggled. "And mine, too."

Madison smiled. "Of course."

"Do you know what you're getting this year for presents?" Aimee asked, skipping down the sidewalk and leaving little snow footprints behind. "I asked for new toe shoes."

"I know my mom got me some new cleats for soccer," Fiona said. "And I asked for a Discman, but I don't know if I'll get one."

"What about you, Madison?" Aimee asked.

"Who knows," Madison said. "I asked for some computer software. And some clothes, of course. But usually Mom takes me shopping after the holidays when all the sales happen."

"What are you giving your parents?" Aimee asked. "My brothers and I got my mom a one-year membership at the yoga center."

"I don't know what to get," Fiona said. "Chet and I can't agree on the right gift. I wanted to make them dinner so we wouldn't have to blow a lot of money. We don't have that much allowance saved."

As they were talking, Madison realized that she hadn't even thought about what she would get Mom or Dad for the holidays. She'd been so worried about her ski trip and Mrs. Romano and the Winter Jubilee concert and everything else at school that she'd forgotten to buy gifts.

"What about you, Maddie?" Aimee pressed.

"I want to get them a snow globe," Madison blurted.

"Huh?" Aimee said, stopping in her tracks. "A what?"

"Did you say snow globe?" Fiona asked.

Madison nodded. "Mrs. Romano, the woman I visit at The Estates, told me this story about this snow globe she has on her dresser. It represents friendship and love and—"

"A snow globe?" Aimee interrupted.

Fiona was bending down to the sidewalk to pick up some snow.

"Maddie, I don't get it," Aimee said. "You have to get a better present than that."

"Heads up!" Fiona said, hurling a mini-snowball at Aimee. It exploded on Aimee's wool coat. The two of them dashed off down the street—armed and *wet*.

Madison blinked at the gray sky and took a deep, cold breath. She wrapped the orange scarf Mrs. Romano had loaned her tightly around her neck and imagined the snowy days long ago when Mrs. Romano may have worn it herself. Did she have snowball fights back then?

And what was wrong with snow globes, anyway? Madison thought they were romantic. Aimee and Fiona just didn't get it.

Madison wondered what Mrs. Romano would be doing for the holidays. What would her kids be getting *her* for Christmas? Nurse Ana said the Romano family hadn't visited in two years because they lived in Italy or some other faraway place. Madison felt woozy just thinking about that. She couldn't imagine living so far away from either parent—even if they were both fighting.

When they turned the corner to Fiona's house, Aimee chased after Fiona to stop there, too.

"Aren't you walking the rest of the way?" Madison asked her.

Aimee shrugged. "I just have to stop and get this book I left at Fiona's. I mean, you can wait if you want . . ."

Madison shook her head. "I have to get home. You know that."

"So I'll see you later then, okay?" Aimee said. "E me."

Fiona waved. "See you later, Maddie. Let's talk later tonight."

As Madison walked away she felt her stomach flip-flop. Were Aimee and Fiona becoming better friends *without* Madison? Or was Madison just being paranoid? She *had* been spending a lot of time away for volunteering. Was that how the switch happened?

Walking along the empty winter sidewalk, Madison realized that understanding her BFFs or her family took a lot of work—especially around the holidays. Would she ever get it? She reknotted the scarf and hurried home to Blueberry Street.

By the time she arrived on her front porch, the snow had either blown away or turned to instant slush. Madison kicked a little off her shoe and went inside. Naturally, Phin rushed to the door.

"Stop panting, Phinnie," Madison said, trying to calm him down. "I know you're happy to see me, but—"

"Hi, Maddie," Mom said, walking into the hallway. "I just got off the phone with Gramma Helen. She sends you her love."

Madison dropped her orange bag onto the floor, took off her wet shoes, and plopped onto the living room sofa.

"Mom, can we talk?" she asked.

Mom plopped down next to Madison. "Sure, what about?" she said.

"How come you never told me that much about Grampa Max?" Madison asked.

"Oh," Mom replied. "He was a sweet man."

"That's *all* you remember about him?" Madison said. "That's so lame, Mom."

"Okay, let me think. Just before you were born, Grampa Max used to make me things. He built me a rocking chair and footstool. You know the one I have in the bedroom. He painted my name and your father's name on it. He was going to paint your name, but . . ."

Mom looked into Madison's eyes.

"You know the end. He died right before you were born," she said.

Madison curled into her mom's side and looked up at her face. "So what happened?" she asked. "When he died, I mean."

"It was very sad. Max was like a dad to me, too,"

97

Mom admitted. "I missed him for a long time. We named you Madison in honor of him, with the letter M."

"Tell me more," Madison pleaded.

"The main thing about Grampa Max was that he always gave of himself—in his own way. It's so important to give to people you care about. He knew what to say at all the right moments. . . ." Mom's voice trailed off. "Unlike your father, who is always—"

"Mom!" Madison yelped. "Why do you have to say that about Dad?"

Mom covered her mouth. "It slipped out. I'm sorry."

"It's always slipping out," Madison said. "Dad isn't such a bad guy, is he? Why did you marry him if you think that? Why do you always have to tell me things like that?"

"Maddie, don't worry. I loved him," Mom said. "You know that. Your father and I can be perfectly civil to one another."

"Then why have you been fighting for the last few weeks?" Madison asked.

"Fighting?" Mom chuckled.

"Yes, and every time you mention him, you get annoyed," Madison said.

"We have not been fighting," Mom said.

Madison rolled her eyes. "Some Christmas," she muttered under her breath. "What a joke."

"What did you say?" Mom asked. "Maddie, I really think—"

"Mom, since you say giving is so important, then will you give me something?" Madison asked.

"Of course I will. What is it, honey bear?"

"Will you go to the Winter Jubilee concert—"

Mom interrupted. "Of course I will! You know that!"

"No, no. I wasn't finished. Will you go to the Winter Jubilee concert—with Dad?" Madison asked. "I already asked him and he said he would have no problem going with you."

Mom closed her eyes and sighed. "Madison," she said slowly. "You know that I can't do that."

"Why not?" Madison asked, sitting upright. "You just said—"

"Don't play games, Maddie," Mom said. "Okay? Maybe your dad and I are not getting along all that great right now, but I don't wish to force the issue."

Madison stood up and backed away from Mom. She picked up her bag and turned toward the staircase.

"Madison, come back here," Mom said. "We didn't finish talking."

"Yes we did." Madison shot Mom a look and went upstairs anyway.

"MADDIE!" Mom shouted. "Come back right now."

But Madison was already at the top of the stairs

with Phin following close behind. She scooped up the dog, scurried into her bedroom, and slammed the door.

Madison pressed an ear to the door, waiting for the sound of Mom's footsteps. Was she coming up? Madison regretted having mentioned the concert. She'd wanted to ask for days, even when she knew what Mom's answer would be: NO.

But she still hoped it might be different.

"MADDIE!" Mom's voice echoed all through the house. "Madison Francesca Finn! I want to talk to you!"

Madison crawled onto her bed with Phin and pretended not to hear.

These holidays were getting less and less cheery by the minute.

Chapter 9

From: Bigwheels
To: MadFinn
Subject: Parents
Date: Thurs 13 Dec 1:14 PM

I'm home sick from school! I have a
fever for 3 days and my nose looks
like a tomato. Have you been sick
at all this winter? I think the flu
stinks.

:-~l

So I guess IOU an apology for not
writing sooner, especially since
it sounds like ur having parental
meltdown a little bit. Sorry about
that. I know what it's like, for
sure. But it seems so funny for

your parents to still be mad at each other when they already got divorced, right?

I think you should stop worrying so much about them. At least you don't have to listen to them argue anymore. You just hear one side and then the other. That's a little bit better than eavesdropping on screaming matches. That's what I listen to sometimes.

Can u ignore them? I mean it is their problem and not yours, right? My head is all stuffed from my cold so maybe my brain is clogged and I can't come up with the greatest advice. Write back and tell me what happens with the concert. I hope they both do go. It's the holidays— they have to be there! Good luck.

Yours till the nose blows,

Victoria aka Bigwheels

P.S. That lady at the place ur volunteering sounds so nice. I'm sure she'll love the concert at least.

Madison was relieved to finally hear back from her keypal. She'd been waiting for days. She hit REPLY immediately.

From: MadFinn
To: Bigwheels
Subject: Re: Parents
Date: Thurs 13 Dec 4:24 PM

I just got home from school and singing practice for the Jubilee concert and I got ur e-msg. THANX SOOOO MUCH. It couldn't have come @ a better time. My mom was just in my room a minute ago acting all normal and completely forgetting the fact that we had this HUGE fight last night. I didn't talk to her @ breakfast before school this morning and barely said hello when I came home.

To make life even wackier, my BFFs are acting distant around me these days and I don't know why. Do you ever feel like friends suddenly like each other better than they like you? Aimee and Fiona are acting like they're the best buds and I'm the third wheel.

Aren't the holidays supposed to be

the time when everyone is NICER to one another? Not in my universe I guess. BTW: I've been so busy that I dunno what is going on with that guy Hart either. Sometimes I get this vibe that he likes me, and then he talks to some other girls. Whatever! I'm off to do my homework!

Hope ur cold gets better soon. Don't blow it (ha ha).

I will write back with concert news.

Yours till the candy canes,

Maddie

Madison hit SEND and headed for the bigfish-bowl.com home page. She noticed that the site had colorful articles posted on holiday crafts and cooking. Maybe there would be an idea for Mom or Dad's gift on the site? Madison needed to think of something clever—fast.

She could hear Mom talking on the telephone downstairs with someone from work. Was Bigwheels right? Could she just ignore Mom and Dad?

Madison opened her orange bag and took out

her blank loose-leaf notebook. She'd scribbled notes to herself earlier that day.

Math pgs. 45 and 92—turn in
   problem sets!!!
Send e-mail to Gramma Helen.
Get gifts for M & D.
Look up Alzheimer's.

She had every intention of finishing her homework first, but Madison grew distracted by the other items on her list. She opened the bigfishbowl.com search engine and plugged in the word *Alzheimer's*. It was hard to spell.

Up popped a list.

```
1 - 10 of about 1,000,000. Search
took 0.13 seconds.
```

Time to surf.

The first site Madison clicked was the "official" site for the Alzheimer's Association. Its busy home page directed Madison to a FAQ page. She knew that meant "Frequently Asked Questions." Exiting that screen, Madison selected a new site . . . and then another one. Web pages were listed in foreign languages like French and Japanese. The amount of information was overwhelming. Madison was not quite sure what to read first.

Phinnie had nestled his warm little pug body in between Madison's ankles, his favorite spot to fall asleep while she did her homework each night. Unfortunately, as Madison leaned over to pet him, she hit the RESET button on her computer by mistake.

"Bummer!" she cried, waiting impatiently for the laptop to boot up again. When the screen came up, she logged onto bigfishbowl.com once more.

But before she could go back to the Alzheimer's search pages, Madison's buddy list popped up. It informed her with a *beep* that she had friends online.

"Who's in the fishbowl?" Madison asked Phinnie, who had jumped into her lap. Awkwardly, Madison pressed keys and checked around to see who else was online. Maybe Bigwheels?

```
BUDDY ONLINE

Balletgrl
DantheMan
Suresh00
TheEggMan
Wetwinz
```

Her keypal wasn't there, but a bunch of other friends were. Dan, Egg, Suresh, Aimee, and Fiona had logged on. Madison's BFFs were in a chat room all by themselves.

"I can't believe it! They're in a chat room and didn't invite me again?" Madison said out loud. But instead of leaving Aimee and Fiona alone online like she had the previous time, Madison decided to surprise them. She'd show up in the chat room—invited or not.

```
<Wetwinz>: I cant believe she
   doesn' t know
<Balletgrl>: whew
<Wetwinz>: M was acting weird tho
<Balletgrl>: w-e, DGT it' ll be fine
<Wetwinz>: Maddie!
```

Madison thought that until she said something to the other members in the room, she would remain invisible. But the moment she entered the chat room her name popped up on the screen—flashing red.

Her BFFs recognized it immediately.

```
<Balletgrl>: OMG! Maddie?
<MadFinn>: hi u guys
<Wetwinz>: what r u doing here???
<Balletgrl>: that is so crazy!!!
<MadFinn>: I was just checking email
   and I saw u were online so I came
   into the lobby
<Wetwinz>: did u c what we were
   saying
```

```
<Balletgrl>: DID u C?
<MadFinn>: not really? Y?
<Wetwinz>: just wondering
<Balletgrl>: CSL!!!! This is soooo
    random
<MadFinn>: Y didn't u ask me to
    chat?
<Balletgrl>: duh maddie we didn't
    know ur online
<Wetwinz>: were just talking about
    math problems right Aim? Ur not
    in our class n e way
<MadFinn>: ok well what were u
    REALLY talking about?
<Wetwinz>: what I said
<Balletgrl>: Maddie its no biggie
```

Madison couldn't understand why they didn't just include her in their conversation. Why couldn't they just tell her the truth?

```
<Wetwinz>: talk now
<MadFinn>: no I have to go
<Wetwinz>: r u ok?
<Balletgrl>: don't go!!!
<MadFinn>: *poof*
```

She could feel tears welling up in her eyes, but Madison quickly grabbed a tissue and wiped them. From the moment she had entered the chat room, Madison sensed it was a mistake. Not only had

Aimee and Fiona been inside the room alone—but they were there talking about Madison.

Madison shut down the computer and ran downstairs to the living room phone. She needed to talk to someone. Mom was out of the question. Who else could she call?

Egg. He'd snap her out of this.

She grabbed a can of root beer from the refrigerator and planted herself on the sofa. She'd just picked up the phone and was about to dial—when she heard voices. Mom was on the extension.

"Fran, I wish you would just listen to me," a man said.

Dad.

"Jeff, I have had enough of this. You promised, you broke your promise. Now I think you owe her a little more than an e-mail apology," the woman said.

Mom.

Madison moved to replace the receiver and get off the phone. From the tone of their voices, the conversation wasn't going very well. She didn't want to hear more talk about the ski-trip-gone-bad or school or other subjects that Mom and Dad liked to argue about.

But she didn't hang up.

For some reason Madison stayed on the phone, holding her breath and listening closer. She was eavesdropping for the second time in one day.

"Enough!" Mom screamed. "I don't want to have

109

this conversation, Jeff. Not again. As it is, Madison thinks we're fighting."

"I know," Dad said. "She talked to me at dinner."

"Oh really! And I suppose you blame me? Do you and your girlfriend have something to say about it?" Mom said.

"Where is this coming from, Effie?" he asked.

Mom sighed into the receiver. "Don't call me Effie. You haven't called me that nickname since we split. Look, I really DON'T want to fight, okay?"

"Then what should I do about the vacation?" Dad asked her.

Madison had the urge to sneeze. She bit her lip hard so she wouldn't give herself away, but there was a pause in the conversation. Had Mom and Dad heard something?

"Hello?" Mom's voice sounded louder than loud in Madison's ear. "Hello? Hello? Must be the phone line."

"There's no one on this end," Dad said.

"You realize, Jeff, that this vacation wouldn't have been a problem if you'd only saved more money."

"Don't bring THAT up all over again," Dad said.

"Why not?" Mom said. "It's a part of the picture, Jeff."

Dad sighed. "Francine . . ."

"And Madison tells me that you think it's a good idea if we attend this holiday Winter Jubilee concert together. . . ." Mom said. "How could you tell her that and get her hopes up?"

"Why not? She wants us to go. It's one night for two hours. I think that's only fair," Dad replied.

"What do you know about fair?" Mom said. "Canceling that vacation, Jeff—was that fair?"

"Fran, let's not talk in circles like this," Dad said. "I said I was sorry. What more do you want from me?"

"How else are you misleading her? Why was Maddie asking about your father the other night? How did the subject of Max come up?" Mom snapped.

"Fran, I won't talk about this," Dad said. "Not when you're angry."

"Why not, Jeff?" Mom pushed. "I feel like I'm in this alone and—"

"STOP! IT!" Madison screamed into the receiver. She hadn't meant to say anything. It just flew out.

The phone line went silent.

"Maddie?" Dad's voice croaked.

"Madison? Are you on the phone?" Mom asked.

"Yes," Madison said. "And I heard everything."

Dad exhaled and Mom let out a little gasp.

"Madison," Dad said, clearing his throat.

"How can you tell me you don't fight? 'Don't worry, Maddie,' you both said to me. 'We don't fight!'" Madison shouted.

"Madison, you shouldn't have heard this—" Mom started to say.

"We were only discussing—please, listen—" Dad tried to finish.

"You were FIGHTING!" Madison said. She didn't want to listen anymore.

"Honey bear," Mom said gently. "Get off the line and come into my office. We can talk more in here."

"No." Madison sniffled into the phone.

"Then let me come over there and we'll sort this out," Dad said.

"No." Madison sniffled again.

"Maddie, I really think that we should all talk—"

"NO!" Madison yelled. "I just don't understand. Why do you two have to act this way? It's Christmas. Why can't we be nice together and have a tree and open presents and eat cookies? Why do I have to be split down the middle? Why?"

"Split down the middle?" Mom said. Now her voice sounded sad.

"Maddie—" Dad choked up.

Madison slammed down the phone and ran back upstairs to her room. She knew this time Mom would be up right away and she was desperate to barricade herself inside the door—or at least under the covers. Phin tagged along, of course.

She ripped off a piece of her loose-leaf and scribbled across the middle: KEEP OUT! DO NOT ENTER! Then she taped it to her door and turned the inside lock,

even though Mom had said never to lock her bedroom door.

Madison went directly to her laptop and opened
a file.

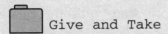 Give and Take

Rude Awakening: 'Tis the season to be
jolly? NOT. For some reason, this winter is
turning into a frost cause.

I am boycotting the school Winter
   Jubilee concert.
I am boycotting Christmas.
I am boycotting my BFFs.
I am boycotting my parents.

"Maddie," Mom whispered outside Madison's
bedroom door.

Knock, knock.

"Please let me in, honey bear," Mom said again,
continuing to knock.

Phin toddled over to the door and sniffed around
when he heard Mom's voice. He scratched at the
floor.

"You have to talk to me sometime," Mom said
softly from behind the door.

Madison hit SAVE and closed her laptop.

"I don't feel like talking," Madison said. But she
opened the door anyway.

Mom stood there holding a plate of fruit. "Peace offering?" Mom said.

Madison looked down at the plate, looked back up at Mom, and then burst into tears. "I'm so sorry!" she wailed.

"Let's sit down," Mom said, guiding Madison over to the bed. "Why don't you tell me what's really going on."

Chapter 10

"Oh, sweetie," Mom said, handing Madison another tissue. She readjusted her position on the bed, and Madison fell headfirst into Mom's lap.

She'd told Mom about Ivy and the drones making fun of her; and about Fiona and Aimee ignoring her.

"I didn't mean to listen in on the phone or to yell," Madison said. "I hope Dad isn't mad at me."

"Honey bear, no one is mad," Mom said. "Not Dad, not me—"

"*I* was mad," Madison admitted. "I was SO mad."

Mom sighed. "You can talk to me," she said. "Rather than letting things get to the boiling point."

"I tried talking, Mom," Madison said, lifting her head. "But when it comes to Dad, you always change the subject. And then you try to tell me I'm worried for nothing."

"Maddie," Mom asked, "what do you want, exactly?"

"I told you. I want you and Dad to come to my Winter Jubilee concert together," Madison said.

Mom grabbed Madison gently. "Why is this so important to you?" she asked.

Madison shrugged. "It just is. Can't you do this one thing because I'm asking you? Because it's the holidays?"

Mom took a long breath. "Maddie," she said. "Let me think about it."

At that moment, Phin jumped up on the bed to investigate. He could usually tell when something was wrong—like now. Madison grabbed his little body and rubbed her nose into his coarse fur.

"Did you hear what Mom said, Phinnie?" Madison exclaimed. "Do you mean it, Mom? Cross your heart and stick needles in your eyes?"

"Yes, except for the needles part," Mom said, chuckling. "But I'm not making any promises, so don't get too excited, okay?"

"Oh, Mom, thanks," Madison said, throwing her arms out for a big hug.

Mom handed Madison the phone.

"Why don't you call your father now and tell him you're feeling better," Mom suggested. "And come downstairs when you're done. Maybe we could bake some cookies after dinner. I bought bittersweet chocolate and other special ingredients."

By the time Madison called his apartment, Dad had already left. She recorded a long message on his answering machine.

"Hey, Dad, it's me, Madison. Um . . . I'm calling and it's almost seven o'clock now and I really wish you were there so I could tell you in person that I am sorry for picking up the phone and then getting all upset and making you and Mom upset, too. Are you there? Dad? Well, when you get this message you will know how bad I feel. Please call me right away when you get back in, okay? Are you having dinner with Stephanie? I think you said that. I am so sorry again. I love you more than . . . well, I love you, Dad. Call me, please? Please?"

Madison hung up before Dad's machine had a chance to cut her off. She didn't want to hear the long and lonely BEEEEEEP before getting disconnected.

Phin chased his tail around in circles, frisky as ever. He knew that Mom and Madison had patched things up. They headed downstairs to the kitchen.

"Want a chewie?" Madison asked, tossing a rawhide bone his way.

Phin licked his chops and howled. "Rahhhhhhhhhhhhrooooooo!"

Mom had pulled out cookie sheets and cookie cutters already. She took down the bowls from the cabinet.

"What kind should we make?" Madison asked.

117

"I was thinking chocolate chip," Mom said.

"Mmmmmm," Madison said.

"I was also thinking maybe we could make an extra dozen for your friend, at The Estates," Mom suggested. "In honor of the holidays."

Madison smiled. "That is such a great idea, Mom. Except, if we're going to do that, can we make a different kind? Mrs. Romano told me once that she loves gingersnaps."

"Wait!" Mom said, holding up her hand. "I think I remember Gramma Helen had a recipe for gingersnaps. . . ."

Mom took out the old recipe-card box from the shelf and thumbed through for the right one.

"Oh!" Mom exclaimed with a grin. "I forgot. Gramma called them "Fred 'n' Ginger" Snaps—after the movie stars. Do you know them? Fred Astaire and Ginger Rogers?"

Madison shook her head. "I think so, but not really."

Mom grabbed Madison around the waist and turned her around in a waltzing circle. "They were dancers. We'll have to rent an old black-and-white movie sometime with them. *Top Hat* is one of my favorites."

"Okay, Mom," Madison said, breaking away with a giggle.

"Sorry," Mom said, squeezing Madison around the middle. "I get carried away sometimes."

After preheating the oven and measuring the ingredients, Mom and Madison mixed everything together and rolled out the gingersnap cookie dough. Mom had star and moon cookie cutters that Madison pressed into the dough and slid onto the cookie sheet. After the baking was done, they cooled the snaps and wrapped them in blue tissue paper Madison found in her box of paper scraps. Mom added a long, yellow grosgrain ribbon that Madison tied into a bow around the paper. She added a small, homemade card with stars and moons drawn all over the front. The card read FOR MRS. ROMANO WHO IS A STAR TO ME. LOVE, MADISON. She thought about adding flowers to match Mrs. Romano's room at The Estates, but decided to put art that matched the cookies instead.

"That Mrs. Romano is going to be so happy," Mom said, washing down the countertop. "You have to tell Gramma Helen we made these."

Madison bit into one of the cookies from the chocolate-chip batch. "Thanks for suggesting it, Mom. I'm glad we talked."

The phone rang and Mom grabbed it.

"Maddie," she said, handing the phone over. "It's Fiona."

Madison picked up the phone. "Hello? What's up?"

"I can't do my history homework!" Fiona wailed into the phone. "How are you?"

"I'm okay. Mom and I just made cookies."

"Yum! I wish I could come over and eat some," Fiona said. "But it's getting late."

"Yeah, I guess," Madison said. "Did you just call to say hi?"

"Yeah, I guess," Fiona replied. "I didn't really see you so much today in school."

Madison could hear boys talking in the background.

"Who's over there?" Madison inquired.

"Drew, Dan, Egg . . ." Fiona said, her voice softening. "They're playing video games."

"Anyone else?" Madison asked.

"No. Hart was supposed to come, but he has the flu."

"Oh," Madison said, trying not to sound like she cared. But she had noticed him missing that day at school.

"Maddie?" Fiona asked. "What's your favorite color?"

"Huh?" Madison asked. "Orange. You know that."

"Oh yeah, I forgot," Fiona said.

"Since when do you care about my favorite color?" Madison asked.

"And your lucky number is thirteen, right?" Fiona asked.

"What's going on? Are you taking a poll or something?" Madison said.

120

"No," Fiona said. "I was just reading this numerology thing in a magazine and—"

"Numerology? So what's *your* lucky number?" Madison asked back.

Fiona thought for a minute. "Nine," she said. "Anyway, I have to go."

"Wait," Madison said. "Aren't you going to tell me?"

"Tell you what?" Fiona asked.

"About the number thirteen," Madison said. "What does it mean in numerology? Am I destined for true love, or lots of money, or what?"

"Can I e-mail it to you? I have to run," Fiona said.

"You have to go? Already?" Madison asked. She wondered if Fiona was rushing off the phone to go call Aimee.

"I still haven't done my homework," Fiona said.

"Oh. Want to hang out tomorrow after school?" Madison asked.

Fiona said she would, but then Madison remembered she couldn't meet anyone the next day.

Tomorrow was the next after-school trip to The Estates.

The flu was going around seventh grade. On Friday, Hart was still out sick. So was Ivy. That meant Madison was taking the bus to volunteering without her crush or her enemy.

Madison had the stars and moons cookies tucked

121

inside a box inside her orange bag, and she kept checking to make certain they would not get smashed before she got there.

Since the group was smaller this time, Nurse Ana cut the orientation meeting short. Everyone disappeared off to the rooms. Madison raced to see Mrs. Romano, but she wasn't there. A nurse's aide was in the doorway.

"Eleanor Romano . . ." a nurse's aide read from a chart. "She is in with Dr. Jacobs right now. Mr. Lynch suggested that you meet her in the waiting room."

Madison and the aide walked around a few corners to a small waiting room with high back chairs. The Estates had doctors right on the premises. A low coffee table was covered in copies of *National Geographic* and some magazine Madison had never heard of called *AARP*. The fine print said that meant "American Association of Retired Persons." Madison flipped through a copy.

"I have to check on someone. Nurse Ana should be by in a moment," the aide said, stepping back into the hallway.

Madison picked up another magazine.

"Annette?" Mrs. Romano said. She came out of the doctor's suite with her walker looking a little pale. "Annette, is that you?"

Madison twisted around to see the person Mrs. Romano was speaking to.

But there was no one there except Madison.

"Mrs. Romano?" Madison said. She took her by the arm. "I just came to visit. I brought you some cookies."

She showed Mrs. Romano the blue-and-yellow package.

"Oh, thank you, Annette," Mrs. Romano said. "I am so happy to see you again."

Madison smiled. Why had Mrs. Romano called her by the wrong name *three times*?

"I'm not Annette," Madison said softly.

"Oh, dear, I know that," Mrs. Romano said, nodding. "You look wonderful today. My scarf looks good on you."

"Um . . ." Madison stammered. "Should we go back to your room now?"

Mr. Lynch appeared inside the doorway. "Maddie!" he cried. "I looked for you after orientation. I see you met up with Mrs. Romano. Hello, Eleanor."

"Um . . . Mr. Lynch," Madison whispered, pulling him over to the side. "Mrs. Romano thought I was someone else just now."

Mrs. Romano didn't hear. She was too busy opening up the cookies.

"Someone else?" Mr. Lynch whispered back. "Who?"

"Annette," Madison said.

"Ahhh. That's her daughter," he said. "Unfortunately, Annette Romano hasn't come to visit in a

123

few years though, as you know. Sometimes Eleanor calls other people by her daughter's name by mistake. It's partly the Alzheimer's and partly—well, she's just a little sad at the holidays. She wishes her real daughter were here, I think."

"Doesn't she remember *me*?" Madison asked.

Mr. Lynch nodded. "Of course she does. Why don't we walk to her room together?"

Madison nodded and they proceeded down the hall.

Halfway there, Mrs. Romano turned around. "Madison?" she said. "I can't believe you remembered that gingersnaps are my favorites."

Madison looked up and smiled. "Do you like them?" she asked, happy to hear her real name.

Mr. Lynch smiled, too. "Can I leave you two alone together now?" she asked and turned back down the hall.

Madison nodded again. "Thanks," she said, waving.

Mrs. Romano huffed. "Leave us alone together? Well, of course you can leave us alone together! What do you think—I bite?"

She squeezed Madison's shoulder as if they were in on the joke together.

Madison giggled.

"Have I ever told you the story about my snow globe?" Mrs. Romano asked.

Of course, Madison had heard it before.

"I think so," Madison said. "But I would love to hear it again."

"I'm so glad you're my friend," Mrs. Romano said as they walked inside. "I can't think of a better way to spend a Friday afternoon."

Chapter 11

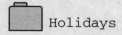 Holidays

Friday turned out great. Mrs. Romano loved the cookies. She added another bird picture to her wall. We hung it up together.

On Saturday I went to another hockey game with everyone. Our team played the Rockets. We lost. Hart is still sick with the flu but he played anyway. Egg was acting like a moron, as usual. Drew was nice. He said he'd make a goal for me, whatever that means. He always says stuff like that. But he didn't make any goals. Neither did Hart. Luckily Ivy wasn't there drooling over him.

Aimee and Fiona sat together at the game, but they weren't ignoring me. At first. Then we rode home together and even though I was sitting in between them, they laughed the whole time like they were sharing some private joke and I was not invited. What's that about?

Rude Awakening: If I'm in the middle, then why do I feel so left out?

On Friday Mom promised—well, half-promised—that she'd go to the Winter Jubilee concert with Dad, but now she didn't mention it all weekend. I'm worried that she won't—and I don't want anyone to tell me to stop worrying. Why did I get my hopes up in the first place? I will probably be the only kid at the concert without both parents there. I know it.

Oh yeah—and I heard on the TV that the weather forecast now says NO SNOW AT ALL!

Excuse me, but what good are the holidays without snow?

"Madison, are you going to school today or what?" Mom asked. She rattled a few dishes as she unloaded the dishwasher.

Madison quickly hit ESCAPE, which turned on her screen saver. A photograph of a baby snow leopard filled the monitor screen.

"I lost track of time," Madison explained as she brought her cereal dish over to the sink and shut down her laptop.

Mom tapped her foot. "This is getting to be a habit with you, my dear." The clock said 7:50 A.M.

Despite the "no snow" forecast, the wind was blustery outside. Mom offered to give Madison a quick ride to school so she wouldn't have to walk.

"I can't believe it's the holiday season again," Mom said as they pulled out of the driveway. "Where does the time go?"

"Mom, you're not going to go to the Winter Jubilee concert with Dad, are you?" Madison asked.

"Whoa," Mom said. "You're got a lot on your mind this morning. Where did that question come from? I told you I would think about it."

"For how long?" Madison asked. She stared out the car window at the other houses in the neighborhood. Everyone had put up decorations by now. Some homes had icicle lights hanging from the roofs while others had plain old pine wreaths hanging on the front doors. As they drove along, Madison counted two plastic reindeer, four golden angels, and fourteen big red bows.

"Madison, you have to be patient about the concert," Mom mumbled. She pointed to the house on the corner. "Hey, did you see what the Emersons did with their front lawn this year?"

Madison had seen it while walking Phin that week. In the yard, they set up a Santa's workshop, complete with elves, Santa and Mrs. Claus, and a giant sleigh covered in gifts that lit up. *Everything* lit up.

"They must have to pay a lot for electricity," Madison said.

"I heard that Jake Emerson hires an electrician to come every year and do special hookups," Mom said.

Madison wondered why someone would spend so much money on decorations. At their house, Mom had put up a tree, a wreath, and a few candles in the windows. That was the extent of their decorating. They had yet to take the ornaments down from the attic to decorate the tree.

"When are we doing the tree?" Madison asked.

"We'll decorate on Christmas Eve," Mom said. "Just like always."

"But it won't really be like always, Mom," Madison said. "Not really."

Madison gazed out the window silently as Mom pulled up to the school parking lot.

"Well, have a nice day," Mom said, trying to sound chipper. "You'd better hustle. It's after eight. We'll talk more later, okay?"

Madison kissed Mom on the cheek and ran toward the front steps so she would make it on time. She caught up with Fiona and Chet on the way inside.

"Yo, Maddie!" Chet bellowed. "What's up?"

"Upstairs, upset, uptown . . ." Madison said.

It was a bad joke, but Fiona giggled.

"Yeah, later for you," Chet said with a pretend look of disgust. He chuckled and rushed ahead to his homeroom.

Fiona followed him, waving back at Madison. "See you at lunch," she said.

Madison entered her homeroom to find Ivy parked next to the seat where Madison usually sat.

"Hey," Ivy said, acting a lot friendlier than the last time they had spoken.

Madison slid into her seat. "Hey, yourself," she said.

"How was The Estates last Friday?" Ivy asked. "I was so bummed that I missed seeing Mrs. Wood. I called her up and said I had the flu."

"Oh yeah?" Madison said, not sure whether or not she should believe Ivy. "Are you feeling better now?"

Ivy coughed for effect. "A little bit. I'm still on antibiotics though."

A voice blared over the loudspeaker. It was Miss Goode, the assistant principal. She always seemed to have trouble making announcements. Egg called her Ol' Yeller.

"ATTENTION, ATTENTION, MAY I HAVE YOUR ATTENTION?"

A kid in the second row yelled back, "YES, YOU CAN!" and everyone burst out laughing. But Mr. Gibbons, Madison's homeroom teacher, clapped his hands to quiet everyone down.

"ATTENTION! WOULD ALL MEMBERS OF SEVENTH GRADE PLEASE REPORT TO THE ASSEMBLY FOR A SPECIAL TALK FROM PRINCIPAL BERNARD. THANK YOU."

The loudspeaker's crackling static sent a shiver down Madison's spine.

Mr. Gibbons clapped his hands together again. "Okay, everyone, let's line up. You heard the announcement."

Everyone filed into the hallway and then headed for the main assembly.

"Long time no see!" Fiona cried out when she spotted Madison. "Like five minutes ago."

Aimee linked arms with Madison on the other side. "What is this assembly about?" she grumbled.

They sat in a row near Egg, Drew, and Hart. Madison found herself staring at Hart, who was sneezing into a tissue the entire time. Even sick he looked cute.

Principal Bernard took the stage wearing his usual, boring gray suit. He coughed into the microphone. Madison guessed that he had the flu, too.

"Students, I brought you here this morning to talk a little bit about this week's seventh-grade festivities. As you know, this week is Winter Jubilee."

Everyone burst into a round of applause, even the kids who were still half asleep.

"Yes, I think it's a grand time, too," Principal Bernard continued. "And I wanted to make some formal announcements about the activities and events that Far Hills Junior High has planned, since it's our first holiday season together like this. First, I'd like to thank each and every one of you for helping to decorate the classrooms and hallways."

The room applauded again.

"Settle down, settle down," the principal said, holding his hands up. "I would also like to thank the committees dedicated to our goodwill Winter Jubilee events."

Madison glanced over in Ivy's direction and Ivy looked back.

"Now, as I understand it, many of you will be singing in a concert at The Estates tomorrow and at school again on Saturday afternoon. The faculty and administration are so pleased with your participation. Give yourselves a hand for that, boys and girls."

Egg heaved his fist into the air. "Woo-woo!" he said. The room started clapping once more. Even Madison, Aimee, and Fiona were whooping.

"There is a distinct group of students, however," Principal Bernard continued, "who deserve our special attention, and I would like to thank those volunteers who have taken extra time out of their busy schedules to meet with residents of The Estates a few times each week. Let's all give the Adopt-a-Grandparent crew a warm thank-you. I'm talking about . . ."

He read through the list of names.

Madison wormed around in her seat as she usually did when someone called attention to her in a large room. She loved to be recognized, but in smaller ways than this. Madison liked it when her friends paid attention, when Mom and Dad noticed, or when Bigwheels wrote e-mails. Having her name read out to a million other seventh graders (well, 246 to be exact) wasn't Madison's idea of holiday fun.

She glanced over at Ivy again. This time, Ivy shrugged and smiled. The drones didn't seem to notice.

Lucky for Madison's self-consciousness, the assembly didn't last much longer. And the rest of the day flew by just as quickly.

Fiona had to attend a party for the soccer team after school and Aimee had rehearsals for *The Nutcracker*, so Madison walked home alone. When she arrived home from school that afternoon, she raced to check her e-mailbox.

From: Bigwheels
To: MadFinn
Subject: Good Luck
Date: Mon 17 Dec 3:13 PM
Tomorrow is the big day, right? I wanted to send e-mail and wish you LUCK. I know you will sing great (even though you say u can't sing LOL).

Tonight is the seventh night of Hanukkah. Did I tell you I was Jewish? I guessed ur not b/c u were talking about Christmas. Hey that's one thing we don't have in common but that's ok. So far this week I have gotten the coolest Hanukkah gifts like this sweater I wanted and a leather journal (I know u would love that one) and earrings and other smaller stuff. Have you ever been to a menorah-lighting ceremony? We have this AWESOME menorah that my father made in some pottery class he took. Even though he's a real estate agent, I think he wishes he made pottery instead. Anyway, it's painted and pretty and I wish I could invite u over for a ceremony before Hanukkah ends. Y do u live so far?

I was glad to hear that ur Mom will probably go to the concert. U have to let me know what happens!!! Check out the greeting card link on bigfishbowl to read a funny card from me to you. It's under the password 67672. I sent it for extra good luck.

BTW: Are u getting Hart a Christmas or Hanukkah present? Maybe he'll give you something?

FC—Fingers crossed.

Write back soon.

Yours till the light bulbs,

Vicki aka Bigwheels

Madison was about to check the link Bigwheels had sent, when she received an Insta-Message.

JeffFinn>: What do snowmen call
  their kids?

Madison laughed. Dad was Insta-Messaging her with a *joke*? She responded and they started to chat.

<MadFinn>: I give up Dad
<JeffFinn>: Chill-dren HA HA HA
<JeffFinn>: maddie? r u there?
<MadFinn>: that was so funny I
  forgot to laugh
<JeffFinn>: so how's my little
  singer?
<MadFinn>: fine I guess
<JeffFinn>: what's wrong? Isn't the
  concert this coming weekend? I'm
  excited!
<MadFinn>: Too bad mom isn't
<JeffFinn>: she still won't go
  with me?
<MadFinn>: Nothing's changed since
  u talked last week can't u
  convince her?
<JeffFinn>: I don't think so

\<MadFinn\>:   please?
\<JeffFinn\>:   things will get better
\<MadFinn\>:   u mean u both will go—
    but you'll be sitting on opposite
    sides of the room???
\<JeffFinn\>:   things will get better!
\<MadFinn\>:   I know
\<JeffFinn\>:   hey what do u want
    from 0\<|:-}}} this Xmas?
\<MadFinn\>:   um . . . world peace
\<JeffFinn\>:   that's a tall order,
    maddie
\<MadFinn\>:   so? ur a tall guy
\<JeffFinn\>:   I love you, M
\<MadFinn\>:   I love u more
\<JeffFinn\>:   things will get better,
    I promise

Madison wanted to believe Dad. But he was always saying things would get better, even when it didn't feel like they were.

It was fun to joke back and forth, too, but Madison knew that if there really *were* a Santa Claus, she would have made a wish for peace of a different kind—the kind that involved both of her parents.

After disconnecting from the Internet, Madison rummaged through her closet, reviewing the next day's events in her mind. Since tomorrow was the concert at The Estates, she needed a super-cute outfit to wear. Madison considered wearing her long black pants and yellow sweater, but decided that made her look too much like a bumblebee. She thought about her dark blue velvet dress, but that made her look like a prairie girl. Finally, she pulled out her nubby roll-neck sweater with the red-and-green trim, a beet-red corduroy skirt, and mini-boots. (She picked out boots just in case it decided to snow.)

This was the ideal outfit.

She could color-coordinate with her BFFs in the morning.

Chapter 12

From: GoGramma
To: MadFinn
Subject: THE CONCERT
Date: Tues 18 Dec 5:44 AM

Maddie, I'm up at the crack of
dawn, as usual. I have been
thinking about you all weekend long.
Are you nervous about singing in
the concert today? Don't be! You
will be a star, I know. Here is a
little poem a friend gave me once.
I want to share it with you.

I give you all good wishes,
because you are so dear
And pray they will come true,
with happiness so near.

Like a special angel,
you do such caring things,
That you deserve your own
pair of angel wings!

Send me an e-mail message and let
me know how the concert goes. I am
sure your Adopt-a-Grandmother will
be as proud of you as I am.

Love, Gramma

Madison reread Gramma Helen's e-mail again. She had printed it out and stuffed it into her skirt pocket that morning so she could have it with her all day long. Reading the e-mail while sitting on the bus headed for The Estates was like having Gramma right there.

No one else was paying much attention to Madison anyway, so she could read all she wanted. Half of the seventh grade was stuffed into the bus. Everyone was shouting and gossiping and complaining about the fact that it still hadn't snowed outside. The ride to The Estates went by faster than fast—or at least faster than usual. Madison's skin broke out into goose pimples.

Nerves.

Hart Jones, whose nose was still a little red from sneezing and suffering through the flu, ended up sitting across the aisle from Madison. She tried to

139

turn casually and look at his face, but it was hard to shift in the seats without looking too obvious.

Madison did *not* want to look obvious.

"Hey, Finnster," Hart whispered across the bus aisle. "This volunteering gig has been a good time, right?" he said.

Madison smiled. "Right," she said.

"Last week I wasn't so sure. I mean, my guy, Mr. Koppell, wouldn't talk to me for, like, ten minutes. I was so freaked out," Hart explained.

"What happened?" Madison asked, mouth agape.

"Nurse Ana told me he has forgetting spells and then he gets embarrassed," Hart said.

"No way!" Madison shrieked. "That sounds just like Mrs. Romano. She called me by someone else's name."

"Hey, Hart," Ivy said, slinking up the aisle, still within earshot of her trusty drones.

"Hey, Ivy," Hart replied. Madison didn't think he seemed interested, but he still responded nicely.

"What are you two talking about?" Ivy asked.

"YOU!" Egg blurted. He'd been listening.

From across the aisle, Fiona giggled at Egg's remark.

"Well, excuse me," Ivy said. "I was just trying to be nice."

"You were nice," Hart said, recovering. "Egg didn't mean it."

Madison wanted to hit Hart in the head for saying that. After everything he'd heard and seen, how could he *still* be sweet on Ivy? Maybe he prescribed to the same philosophy as Fiona—you get what you give?

Madison looked over at Ivy. "We were really just talking about volunteering, you know," she said.

Ivy smiled. "Oh," she said, heading back to the drones. "Later, then."

The bus pulled into The Estates about ten minutes after that, passing the same rows of drooping winter plants on the way into the entryway cul-de-sac. From inside the bus, Madison shivered.

More nerves.

"I love, love, love that skirt, Maddie," Aimee said as they got up to exit the bus. "I was going to wear one just like it, but it looks so much better on you."

"Nice color," Hart said.

Madison raised her eyebrows. "Really?" she said, starting to laugh. Hart had noticed her skirt?

"WATCH IT!" Egg squealed in her ear. He pushed Madison's back. "Would you move, please?"

"Walter!" Señora Diaz said. "That's quite enough. Get off the bus in an orderly fashion or not at all."

Egg's shoulders drooped as he walked off, leaving his friends giggling behind him. Once again, his mother had embarrassed him. And once again he had to take it.

141

An enormous crowd of Far Hills seventh graders invaded The Estates. Residents who had been milling about in the lobby stopped to stare at the young busload of kids.

"Welcome, everyone! *Buenos días!*" Nurse Ana said, waving her hands in the air.

Mrs. Montefiore threw her arms around Nurse Ana and smiled. "We're so happy to be here. Is the piano all set?"

The kids divided into groups with the different teachers. Slowly, the groups moved inside the door to avoid standing out in the cold.

"Please stay together," Señora Diaz said.

"No monkey business!" bellowed Mrs. Montefiore, taking herself too seriously, as always. She grabbed two kids who were chewing gum.

"Follow me to the auditorium," Mr. Lynch said with a grin. He was wearing a reindeer tie.

Madison, Aimee, and Fiona linked arms and shuffled along behind the boys.

Even though they had been rehearsing for a couple of weeks, the class was still unsure in places about lyrics and tempo. They pushed together on makeshift risers placed on the center of a makeshift stage. When Mrs. Montefiore played a few notes on her pitch pipe and got everyone quieted down for warm-ups, Aimee and Fiona squeezed closer to Madison.

Do, re, mi, fa, sol . . .

Madison could hear all the people who had the best voices. Fiona and Ivy stood out the most. She could hear Hart singing, too. It was one thing he wasn't so great at—but at least they had that in common. Maybe they could mouth all of the words to the songs *together*?

After a few vocal warm-ups, the kids were asked to sit down quietly on the risers while the residents of The Estates filed in. Madison was surprised to see a throng of older men and women vying for the front rows. Everyone was dressed up. She scanned the crowd for Mrs. Romano.

"There's Smokey!" Egg said, waving his arms wildly. Smokey gave Egg the thumbs-up.

Mrs. Holly Wood was seated front row, dead center. Ivy shimmied over to the edge of the stage to say hello.

Other kids waved and hooted at the residents, too.

But Mrs. Romano wasn't there yet.

Madison craned her neck for five minutes, bobbing and weaving among her fellow classmates for a glance at her new friend.

Where had she gone?

"May I have your attention, please?" Nurse Ana spoke up louder than loud. The microphone was broken. "Please give our school volunteers a warm welcome. These fine students have come all the way

143

from Far Hills Junior High to share some of the holi-day spirit with you."

Most of the residents clapped politely. The students stood up tall and began to sing.

Ivy led off with a solo rendition of "Winter Wonderland" while the rest of the chorus hummed and cooed. Madison had to admit that Ivy's voice sounded beautiful. Mrs. Holly Wood cheered when she was done.

Fiona sang a solo, too. She put on a "costume" for it. Mrs. Montefiore loaned her a red, rubber nose and furry brown antlers.

" 'Rudolph the red-nosed reindeer,' " Fiona crooned, " 'had a very shiny nose . . .' "

Madison giggled as the chorus sang backup. Hart even had a guest vocal. He played the voice of Santa.

" 'Rudolph with your nose so bright, won't you guide my sleigh tonight,' " Hart yelled. Everyone laughed.

In addition to other Christmas carols and Hanukkah songs, the seventh graders sang a Kwanza and New Year's tune, too.

"Bravo! Bravo!" Smokey said, jumping up and stomping his feet when they sang their finale, "Sleigh Ride." It was their best number. The whole room liked it so much, they sang along, too.

"Please everyone join us for some refreshments down in the dining area," Mr. Lynch said after the applause died down. "Our resident chef has made us some sweet treats."

Egg and Hart high-fived each other. "FOOD!" they cheered.

Madison turned to Aimee and Fiona. "That went surprisingly well. Your solo was awesome, Fiona."

"Oh my God, TOTALLY," Aimee said. "I couldn't stop listening."

"Let's go walk around," Fiona suggested. "I really want to meet Mrs. Romanoff."

"Her name is Romano," Madison corrected her. "And I don't think she's even here. I didn't see her in the audience."

Madison was wondering, even if her new friend had seen the performance, did Mrs. Romano really know *who* was singing? Was it Madison . . . or Annette onstage?

"MADDIE!" a woman yelled from across the room. "MADDIE!"

Madison looked up to find Mrs. Romano rushing over without her walker. She had her arms outstretched for a hug.

And she had remembered Madison's name.

"Mrs. Romano!" Madison said with a grin. "Did you see it?"

"See it? You children are such a talented bunch!" she proclaimed. "I was tickled. I started singing along with almost every tune, too. Thank you!"

Fiona and Aimee tugged on Madison's shirt

as if to say, "Um . . . hello . . . please introduce us?"

Madison presented her BFFs. Mrs. Romano gushed, telling them how beautiful and talented and smart they all were. Madison blushed. Aimee and Fiona basked in the attention.

"And who was that sweet girl who sang 'Winter Wonderland'?" Mrs. Romano asked.

Aimee winced. "Sweet girl?" she said.

Fiona smiled. "You must mean Ivy," she said.

"Ah! Well, she has a lovely voice, a lovely face, and a lovely name, too," Mrs. Romano said.

Aimee snorted. "Lovely Poison Ivy," she snickered under her breath.

Madison grabbed Mrs. Romano by the elbow. "Are you going for the refreshments?" she asked.

Mrs. Romano shook her head. "I was hoping maybe you could come and visit my room. I have some delicious gingersnaps that need eating," she said, winking. "Can you leave your friends for a few minutes?"

Madison nodded. "Catch up with you guys later?" she said.

Aimee and Fiona said their polite good-byes and went off to the snack room. After getting Nurse Ana and Señora Diaz's permission, Madison sneaked away with Mrs. Romano for fifteen minutes.

Since Madison had last visited, Mrs. Romano had decorated her small room for the holiday season.

She had a miniature Christmas tree placed atop a table, covered in tinsel and little white lights. On the branches of the tree, Madison counted twenty-three birds made from all sorts of materials, from paper and foil to straw and yarn.

"That's beautiful!" Madison remarked. She carefully examined every bird.

"And this is for you," Mrs. Romano said, handing Madison a small gift box. Inside was another bird ornament. This one had real yellow and green feathers on it. "Now you can be a bird lady, too," she said.

"I can't believe this," Madison said. "It's so special."

"And that isn't all," Mrs. Romano said. She reached on her nightstand and revealed another small gift box.

"What's this?" Madison asked.

She opened the package to reveal a snow globe—similar to the one Mrs. Romano had been given by her friend. This one had a snowman inside, too.

Madison wanted to cry, but she started to laugh instead. The concert was a success! She had her own snow globe to prove it.

Madison couldn't wait to tell Gramma Helen that the angel wishes had been luckier than lucky.

Chapter 13

At school the next day, everyone was buzzing about The Estates concert. The seventh graders had received a standing ovation. Mrs. Montefiore was being nice for the first time in weeks.

Kids gossiped in the halls about winter break. Vacation was right around the corner now.

Teachers decorated the halls of Far Hills Junior High with art class collages and paintings. Mr. Duane's photography class spent the month shooting a photo retrospective of sports teams with black-and-white film. For the holidays, he'd framed the photos and hung them in the school lobby. During a break between classes, students gathered in the halls to take a look.

"Look!" Aimee squealed. "It's me! They came to our dance class last month. I remember that!"

Madison saw a photograph of Aimee in her leotard, posing at the barre. She looked pretty and graceful, as always.

From behind them, Chet whistled. "You look hot, Aimee," he said, cracking himself up. Fiona punched his shoulder for saying that, but Aimee thanked him. She wouldn't turn down a compliment from anyone, not even an annoying boy.

"Hey!" Egg cried. "Check this one out. It's from our hockey scrimmage. Hart, you're on the ice, man! Good one!"

In the photograph, Hart had fallen down on his side on the ice. Drew stood over him, stick in the air. It was a great action shot.

"I remember that!" Drew shouted. "I checked you!"

"Couldn't they show me making a goal?" Hart said, smiling. "I look like SUCH an idiot in that picture."

"No you don't," Madison said without thinking.

"Yeah," Hart said. "I do. But thanks anyway, Finnster."

Madison's face flushed. Hart had looked right into her eyes when he said that. How could a look feel more intense than actual touching?

"Hey, Fiona," Drew said. "Where's the picture of you playing soccer?"

Fiona shrugged. "On the cutting room floor I guess. Boohoo."

"They should put up a picture of you singing a solo," Egg said, giving Fiona a HUGE compliment right there in front of everyone. "You were the best one at the concert yesterday."

Madison covered her mouth so she wouldn't smile too obviously. Aimee hid her grin, too. The mutual crush between Egg and Fiona was as transparent as plastic wrap. Something was bound to happen between them sooner than soon. Maybe over winter break? Madison wondered.

"Hey, Maddie, have you decided what you're doing yet for vacation?" Aimee asked aloud. "Are the ski plans back on?"

Madison shook her head. "Not yet. But that's okay."

"Hey, I'm going skiing—if it ever snows!" Hart chimed in. "My parents are taking me and my brother up to Mount Robinson. Have you ever been there?"

Madison's heart sank. "Almost," she said. "I was going to go stay there for a week this winter break, but my dad had a work conflict and my mom didn't want me to go for so long and then he said . . . well . . . forget it."

She stopped talking midsentence. Was anyone listening?

"What a bummer," Hart said.

Madison nodded. "Yeah. I guess." In the two weeks that she was singing in chorus and visiting with Mrs. Romano, Madison had pushed the ski trip into the back of her mind. But now, she felt disappointed all over again.

150

"Actually, my family is going skiing, too," Drew piped up. "To Switzerland. My parents have a reservation at some spa there."

Since Drew was easily the richest kid in class, he flew to ski resorts in Europe while the other kids were visiting tinier mountaintops near Far Hills. It was amazing how normal he acted in school.

"Anyone else want to come to Switzerland?" Drew asked the group. But he was looking straight at Madison when he said it.

Madison laughed in his face. "Yeah, right!"

Aimee leaned over to Madison and Fiona and whispered in her lowest voice. "I think I'm going to marry Drew and travel all over the world. HA! Wouldn't that be awesome?"

"Yeah, right!" Fiona teased.

By now, Madison wasn't really paying attention to Drew or her BFFs. Her gaze had drifted over to Hart, who was busy gabbing with Chet and looking at more pictures on the wall.

Madison wanted to marry *him*.

Brrrrrring.

When the class bell rang, some of the boys rushed off to classes together. Egg grabbed Madison by the elbow.

"You have computer lab now, right, Maddie?" he asked.

Madison nodded.

"I took digital photos of yesterday's concert," Drew said. "And Mrs. Wing wants to put them up on the Web site."

"You're good at writing captions," Egg said, pulling on her sweater. "You have to help us."

Madison shrugged and said good-bye to her BFFs as they disappeared together toward science class. Fiona looked back once, like she wanted to stay with Egg. But he was on his way to Mrs. Wing's classroom.

Madison followed him there. Along the way, she bumped into Ivy and company.

"Ivy," Madison said, ignoring the drones. "You did a really good job singing at The Estates yesterday. Everyone said so."

Joanie made a face.

"Um . . . let's go, Ivy," Rose demanded. "Like, NOW."

Ivy didn't budge. She turned away from the drones.

"That's really nice of you to say that, Maddie," Ivy said. "I mean it. Thanks a lot. You did a good job, too."

Madison remembered Gramma Helen's words and Fiona's words. They were especially true right now.

You get what you give.

"Hurry up!" Egg cried, racing down the hall. "The bell's gonna ring, Maddie."

"See ya," Madison said to Ivy. She glared at the

drones and spun around so she could catch up with Egg. She didn't look back once.

The computer lab was only a few yards away but Madison had to catch her breath as she entered. Drew was already set up at one terminal, downloading digital photos. Madison walked over and began to think up captions for the screen captures.

```
Residents of The Estates ring their
   Jingle Bells
Fiona Waters sings Rudolph the
   Red-nosed Reindeer with a red nose!
Hanukkah coins, candles, and music
   for everyone
Members of the Class Seven chorus
   do the Christmas "wave"
Señora Diaz and Mrs. Montefiore
   enjoy the food
```

"Hey, Maddie!" Egg called out from his computer terminal. He was programming an online holiday poll for students.

"What?" Madison barked back.

"I was just wondering . . . are you going back to The Estates after Christmas is over?" Egg asked.

"Well, yeah," Madison said. "Of course." She hadn't actually thought much about it until now.

"Smokey said I could visit him anytime," Egg boasted.

"Mrs. Romano did, too!" Madison said. "And she

gave me presents, too. An ornament of a bird and a snow globe."

"A snow globe? You mean the thing you shake up?" Egg said. "Why did she give you that?"

Madison explained the whole story. Egg didn't make fun, as Madison expected he would.

"She sounds as nice as Smokey," Egg said. "I think it's good that we got to know them."

"And you didn't want to volunteer at first," Madison said. "Remember?"

Egg laughed. "Yeah, I know—but just because it was my mom. You know the deal. Sometimes she really gets on my case."

The loudspeaker overhead crackled. Madison and Egg stopped to listen.

"ATTENTION! ATTENTION! DUE TO THE SEVERE WEATHER WARNING, PRINCIPAL BERNARD HAS CANCELED ALL AFTER-SCHOOL ACTIVITIES. STUDENTS ARE ASKED TO REPORT TO THE SECRETARY'S OFFICE IF YOU NEED TO CONTACT A PARENT."

Madison and Egg looked at one another.

Severe weather warning?

They ran to the window of the computer lab and looked outside. The sky was a little gray, but nothing spectacular. Other students gathered to look outside, too.

"Kids," Mrs. Wing said. "Please get back in your seats and finish your projects. We can watch for snow a little later."

"Snow?" Madison said. "Since when is it supposed to snow?"

"All day and all night," Mrs. Wing said. "There's a snow advisory in effect. At least that's what I've heard."

"The weather lady said it was going to snow days ago," Madison moaned.

Mrs. Wing laughed. "Oh really?"

"Snow! Snow! Snow!" one kid chanted. Egg, Drew, Lance, and a few other kids in the lab joined in.

Madison gazed out of the window. The sky darkened a little bit, moving together into one giant, gray cloud.

Was this the moment she'd been waiting for all week long?

Since computer lab was the last class of the day, Madison left class and headed straight for the lockers. On the way, she spotted Aimee and Fiona in the halls. They were standing in front of Fiona's locker, acting chummier than chummy. For a moment, Madison didn't even think they'd say hello. They seemed way more interested in each other.

But a second later, Aimee twirled her body around in a circle and waved to Madison. She darted over. Fiona followed behind, giggling.

"Hi, there," Aimee said with a smile.

"Hey," Madison said. "What are you guys up to? I saw you standing there. I didn't think you saw me."

"Of course we saw you," Fiona said, giggling some more.

"What's so funny?" Madison asked.

"We have something to tell you," Aimee said.

Madison gulped. This was it. They were going to tell her that they'd decided they had become better friends and Madison would have to find some new BFFs. . . .

"Tell you? No, we have something to SHOW you," Fiona said, correcting Aimee.

"Oh yeah. Duh," Aimee said, hitting herself in the forehead. "I'm so excited I can't even speak."

"What is it?" Madison asked.

Fiona pulled a gift-wrapped box out from behind her back. "Here!" she proclaimed.

"For me?" Madison said, blinking twice.

Aimee leaned over and gave Madison a big squeeze. "Of course!" she said. "Open it! Open it! OPEN IT!"

"Yeah," Fiona said, thrusting it into Madison's hands. "I can't wait to see the look on your face."

Madison's chest heaved.

This was what Aimee and Fiona had been getting from the lockers?

This was what they had been talking about "together?"

This was the big secret?

Carefully, Madison untied the green ribbon on the package. Little silver bells were knotted at each end of the ribbon so the package made a tinkling noise every time Madison moved.

"Jingle bells!" Fiona said.

"Come on, Maddie," Aimee said. "You're too slow. Rip it open!"

But Madison took her time. The package was wrapped beautifully in red foil paper embossed with little Christmas trees. She peeled back the tape and opened the ends. Inside was a hard box wrapped in a layer of bright orange tissue paper.

"Orange!" Fiona blurted. "Your favorite color, right?"

Madison remembered when Fiona had asked her that question a few days before. Slowly, Madison pulled the tissue away to reveal the gift beneath.

A *collage* box.

"Do you like it? Do you like it?" Aimee asked before Madison even had a chance to respond.

"Like it?" Madison repeated. She took a deep breath and opened her mouth to speak—but no more words came out.

"Maddie?" Fiona asked. "Are you okay?"

Madison looked down at the collage box. Aimee and Fiona had decorated it with words and pictures of the three friends together. On top were the words SUPER FRIENDS 4-EVER. Around the sides, they'd pasted photos of Madison's favorite animals, including Phin and Blossom. And inside, they'd lined the box with felt and fabric. They traced the number "13" on one edge.

"For good luck," Aimee said. "Your lucky number is inside the box!"

"I can't believe this," Madison said dumbly.

Aimee and Fiona squealed. "She likes it!" and threw their arms around Madison. The trio grabbed the rest of their stuff and headed for the door.

"It's snowing!" Aimee said as they crossed the street and wandered away from school together.

Fiona broke into song. "'. . . walking in a winter wonderland . . .'"

As Madison looked up, a few fat flakes landed—*splot!*—on her face. She bent down and slipped the present into her bag so it wouldn't get wet.

"I can't believe you guys made me this present," Madison said. "I went with Mom and bought your presents at the mall."

Aimee and Fiona grinned.

"Well, you ALWAYS make us stuff," Aimee said.

"So it was our turn to make stuff for you!" Fiona said.

Madison sucked in some cold air and let out a little gasp.

You get what you give.

Arm in arm, the three best friends headed for home under the snowy sky.

Chapter 14

When Madison got home, Mom handed her Phin's leash. He needed a quick walk before the weather got any snowier.

Madison grabbed Phin around the middle and pulled on his newest knit sweater. Gramma Helen sent it from a specialty pet store in Chicago. It was dark blue with little snowflakes. Just right for the day's weather.

"Rowrrooooooo!" Phin howled and circled around excitedly, getting his little paws caught in the leash.

Madison grabbed the end and hurried outside.

The streets were busier than usual. People were heading home from work. Kids were still coming back from school. The city services truck drove by and dumped salt along the road to keep it from icing. Its giant plow was raised, but Madison knew that would be put into good use soon enough.

The sky was still light out even through the gray, and the eerie brightness reflected off the flakes of falling snow. It really is a winter wonderland out here, Madison thought. Phin trotted alongside her, stepping lightly since his paws were cold. He stopped to pee and then turned around for home right away.

But Madison picked him up so she could walk back slowly. She wanted to savor every moment of this delicious afternoon. Snow dropped from the sky like powdered sugar. It was like being inside a real-life snow globe.

Madison stopped short in the middle of the wet sidewalk.

A snow globe? That was it!

Her legs picked up the pace and she found herself sprinting toward home, trying not to slip along the way. Madison needed to tell Mom what she was thinking before the sky got any darker or the day got any later. She had something very important to do.

Phin howled.

He loved his bumpy ride in the snow.

"I still don't know about this," Mom said to Madison. They were packed into the car with the heater on full blast.

"It will be okay. I swear it will. I called Nurse Ana like you said and she told me to come over right away," Madison said.

Mom looked over at Madison. Phin, still wearing his sweater, was nestled in her lap.

"Tell me again why building a snowman is so important?" Mom asked.

Madison turned and pressed her nose to the cool glass car window. She gazed at the snow that was falling faster and harder by now.

"Because it is, Mom," Madison said. "Because if I can build a snowman on the lawn while it's still snowing, then it will be like a snow globe and Mrs. Romano loves her snow globe! Don't you get it? When she looks out of the window, it'll be like she's in the middle of it!"

"Honey bear, what are you talking about?" Mom asked. "You're not making any sense."

"You'll see! You'll see!" Madison said. "It will make sense to Mrs. Romano."

Snow gathered in little drifts on the windshield wipers as they drove along. Bit by bit, the snow was piling up everywhere. The weather lady *had* been right when she said a storm was moving it. This was it. But for a storm, Madison thought it felt awfully *pretty* outside.

When Mom finally pulled into the cul-de-sac entryway at The Estates, she put the car into park and Madison pushed open the door.

"I want you to hurry up!" Mom yelled. "We have to head back home before the snow starts falling any harder."

Mom took Phin. She said she would take him for another walk around the property and then check in on Madison's progress making the snowman.

Madison grabbed a large paper bag from the backseat. Then she waved as if to say "yeah, yeah," and disappeared inside The Estates. She had agreed to meet up with Nurse Ana before she went home for the day. It was a little before four o'clock now.

"Hello!" Madison said when she saw Nurse Ana and Mr. Lynch standing together by the front desk.

Mr. Lynch introduced Madison to Frankie, a maintenance man, and explained the "plan." Frankie laughed when he heard it.

"That's the best holiday present anyone could ask for!" he said. "Let me help you! You'll want to have it done before the sky gets any darker now!"

With everyone's blessing, Madison and Frankie headed outside, back into the snow. They walked around to the back of the residential area, directly behind Mrs. Romano's room. Frankie started to roll the bottom part of a snowman's body. Madison rolled the middle part. In only five minutes, they had two thirds of a snowman done.

Madison leaned down to roll the head of the snowman while Frankie smoothed the existing parts.

"Hey, this is fun!" he said, rubbing his gloves along the sides.

Madison laughed. The snow on her nose tickled. Her jeans and her jacket were getting wet, too.

Finally, she lifted the snowball head onto the rest of the snowman.

"Looks good, kid," Frankie said, wiping the wet snowfall from his own forehead. "Whew! Never seen such a nice snowperson."

"And we're not done yet," Madison said. She lifted some objects out of the paper bag she'd dragged from the car. Five black rocks served as buttons and eyes while five smaller rocks formed a smile. A carrot made the nose, just like in the *Frosty the Snowman* cartoons. Madison took out an old black hat she'd found in the basement at home and a fuzzy green scarf that Mom never wore.

"How about these?" Frankie suggested, handing Madison two short branches.

She poked them in for arms and turned toward the sky.

Snow was still falling fast.

The living snow globe was complete.

From across the lawn, Madison heard clapping. Nurse Ana, Mr. Lynch, and Mom were standing by the side of the yard with Phin.

"Bravo!" Mom shouted.

"Let me go get Mrs. Romano," Mr. Lynch said. He went back inside.

Madison turned toward Mrs. Romano's window and waited for the curtain to open. When it finally moved, she held her breath.

Mrs. Romano squinted to see who was out on the lawn. Madison expected she might have thought special birds were paying her a special visit. But Madison waved instead.

"Hello!" Madison yelled. "LOOK!" She pointed to the snowman.

Mrs. Romano cupped her hand over her mouth and squinted again. She shook her head with disbelief and unlocked the window.

"Madison!" she cried. "Is that you?"

"And I brought a friend," Madison said.

Mrs. Romano ducked back behind the curtain. Madison wondered where she had gone, but then she reappeared with something in her hand.

"A friend!" Mrs. Romano said, holding up her snow globe. She started to sniff and wipe her eyes.

Madison trudged over to the window and held her hand out. "Happy holidays," she said.

Mrs. Romano wiped her eyes. "Same to you, my dear," she said, taking Madison's hand.

By now, the sky really was getting darker and Mom wanted to head for home. They went into The Estates for a short visit with Mrs. Romano. She loved meeting Phin the best. He curled up on Mrs. Romano's bed and growled at a stuffed bird she had on her table.

As they were leaving, Mom put her arms around Madison. "That was a very thoughtful thing to do, young lady," Mom said. "I am very impressed."

Madison shrugged. "She doesn't have any family," she said. "And it's important to have your family at this time of year—no matter who they are."

Mom beamed. "I am so lucky to have you for a daughter," she said, kissing Madison's wet head.

"Oh, Mom," Madison said. "Quit getting all mushy."

"You know, I think that these holidays will turn out just right for you, too," Mom said. "You have to trust me on that."

"Well, I'm over the whole winter break ski thing," Madison said. "If that's what you're talking about."

"Look, Maddie, I am very sorry if I said some things that I shouldn't have said about your father this week. I don't want you to feel like you're stuck between us. That's not the way it should be."

Madison nodded. "Whatever, Mom. I know."

"And I've decided that we should go to the concert together," Mom said.

Madison looked up at her with disbelief. "Huh?"

"Your dad and I will be attending the concert tomorrow—to see our one and only daughter *together*."

Madison's jaw dropped. "You mean it?" she asked.

"Of course," Mom said. "It's the spirit of the season.

And it's important to you. I love you, honey bear."

"Thanks, Mom," Madison said.

Now *she* was getting all mushy. They got into the car and headed for home.

After pulling into the Finn driveway, Madison, Mom and Phin walked up the snowy walkway and onto the porch. Phin let loose another wild howl, happy to be back in his own warm stomping grounds. As soon as they went inside, Madison gave the dog a cookie and played toss for a few minutes.

The snow continued to fall outside while everyone settled into a routine.

Phin curled up for a long winter's nap.

Mom stopped into her office to check the message machine.

Madison made a beeline for her laptop.

She logged onto bigfishbowl.com hoping that Aimee or Fiona might be in there so she could tell them what had happened at The Estates. But no one was online right now.

There was mail, however—a LOT of mail. And hardly any of it was junk mail. Madison opened the bigfishbowl mailbox.

FROM	SUBJECT
✉ GoGramma	Re: The Concert
✉ Wetwinz	Sleepover @ my house
✉ Sk8ing Boy	Wanna go skating?
✉ JeffFinn	Ski Trip is ON
✉ Bigwheels	Ur Grrrreat

Gramma had written back responding to Madison's update on the concert. She'd written to her grandmother the day before.

```
From: GoGramma
To: MadFinn
Subject: Re: The Concert
Date: Fri 21 Dec 11:24 AM
```
I am so proud of you, Maddie. I only wish I could have been there to see you sing on Tuesday. I hope that Saturday's concert goes just as nicely. Write to me and tell me what happens? Give Mom and Phin a kiss for me.

Love, Gramma

Next, Madison read mail from Fiona, who had written to Madison and Aimee that afternoon from her home. It was a nice surprise.

```
From: Wetwinz
To: MadFinn; Balletgrl
Subject: Sleepover @ my house
Date: Fri 21 Dec 3:39 PM
```
My mom rocks! She said u guys can come over 4 a sleepover next week. Probably Thurs or sometime after Xmas is over. Can you guys come? Pleeeeeez? We can rent a movie and

everything. LMK as soon as u can,
okay?

U guys r the best BEST friends ever.

xo, Fiona

Madison felt silly for how she'd mistrusted Fiona and Aimee all week long. Of course they were still best pals! Three was definitely not a crowd in their case.

The next piece of mail was an even bigger surprise.

```
From: Sk8ingBoy
To: Bossbutt; Dantheman; TheEggMan;
W_Wonka7; Peace-peep; L8RG8R;
Wetwinz; Wetwins; BalletGrl;
MadFinn; Rokstarr; 0712biggy;
DougLee; B_Foster; SkatrGod;
Kickit88; CharlieX; JK4ever;
Rosean16; Flowr99; LuvNstuff
Subject: Wanna go skating?
Date: Fri 21 Dec 3:50 PM
```
Hey guys. I want to plan a pickup game at the lake over break. Okay? Write back everyone. C U soon.

Even though he hadn't signed it, Madison knew it was from Hart. She recognized the screen name. A lot of the other names weren't as easy to spot, however. She saw the usual suspects: Egg, Drew, Chet, Fiona,

168

Aimee, Dan, Lance, and some other kids from school. A lot of screen names belonged to other seventh graders who were on the hockey team with Hart. And then, of course, he'd invited Ivy, Rose, and Joan.

Oh well, Madison thought. Maybe they wouldn't show up!

She hit SAVE and opened the next message from Dad. Madison was very confused by the subject line at first.

```
From: JeffFinn
To: MadFinn
Subject: The Ski Trip is ON
Date: Fri 21 Dec 4:15 PM
```
I just booked three days at Mount Robinson, Maddie. I worked out the details with your mother. Are you ready to go ski with me? This is a sure thing, sweetheart, so pack your bags. I'll tell you more tomorrow night when I see you at the school concert.

I love you, Dad

Madison read Dad's mail through again just to make sure she understood it perfectly. Her vacation was back on? She gave a little high-pitched squeal right there at her desk. It was too good to be true.

But it WAS true.

The last e-mail was a quick note from Bigwheels, who had written back like Gramma Helen had, congratulating Madison on the successful concert.

Madison hit REPLY right away.

From: MadFinn
To: Bigwheels
Subject: Re: Ur Grrrreat
Date: Fri 21 Dec 5:28 PM
Thanks a lot, but YOU are the one
who's great. Ur e-mails for the
past few weeks have been so
supportive. I am psyched to have u
as a keypal.

It brought me good luck too,
because suddenly everything is
switching all around again. Or
maybe it's just switching back
to normal. My BFFs are back.
They made me this collage box.
It is so nice, I wish I could
show you. And I'm not freaked out
about wasting my winter break n e
more! I have tons of stuff to do.
Other kids asked me to go skating
and shopping and my Dad is even
taking me to ski--only 3 days
but it's better than nothing,
right?